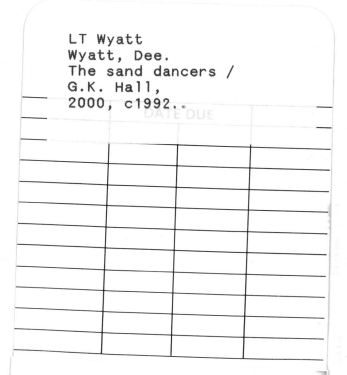

LT Wyatt
Wyatt, Dee.
The sand dancers /
G.K. Hall,
2000, c1992..

DATE DUE

THE SAND DANCERS

Dee Wyatt

Chivers Press • G.K. Hall & Co.
Bath, England Thorndike, Maine USA

This Large Print edition is published by Chivers Press, England, and by G.K. Hall & Co., USA.

Published in 2000 in the U.K. by arrangement with Robert Hale Ltd.

Published in 2000 in the U.S. by arrangement with Robert Hale Ltd.

U.K. Hardcover ISBN 0-7540-3933-1 (Chivers Large Print)
U.K. Softcover ISBN 0-7540-3934-X (Camden Large Print)
U.S. Softcover ISBN 0-7838-8762-0 (Nightingale Series Edition)

The text of this Large Print edition is unabridged.
Other aspects of the book may vary from the original edition.

Set in 16 pt. New Times Roman.

Printed in Great Britain on acid-free paper.

British Library Cataloguing in Publication Data available

Library of Congress Cataloging-in-Publication Data

Wyatt, Dee.
    The sand dancers / Dee Wyatt.
        p.   cm.
    ISBN 0-7838-8762-0 (lg. print : sc : alk. paper)
    1. Large type books.   I. Title.
    [PR6073.Y32S26   2000]
    823'.914—dc21   99–41958

CHAPTER ONE

James Lovell wasn't accustomed to waiting about. People who knew him best would tell you that patience wasn't exactly one of his strongest points, and the fact that the plane was forty minutes late was stretching his short fuse to its limits. He'd been pacing up and down the terminal lounge for the last hour and a half, glancing irritably every couple of minutes at the large round watch on his left wrist, and cursing the gale-force headwinds blustering in from the Atlantic, winds that were causing delays to all the flights in and out of Shannon.

It was suffocatingly hot inside the airport building—someone had gone mad with the central heating controls—and James's long, artistic fingers unfastened the buttons of his dark blue trench-coat, his dark, almost black, eyes scanning the leaden clouds for the smallest speck of a plane.

'How much longer, damn it!' he muttered, glancing exasperatedly again at his watch. It told him it was less than two minutes since his last check.

He hadn't wanted to pick her up anyway. It should have been Mike's job, but Mike had come down with flu, and Enid had gone off somewhere without a word, as usual. There

1

was no one else left to do it, apart from Aunt Harriet, and he couldn't expect her to make the six hour drive to Shannon and back—especially on the hazardous roads through the Caha mountains. Besides, he had a strong feeling that she wouldn't have wanted to do it anyway. She'd left them in no doubt what her thoughts had been of having Leisal Adrian stay with them at Hanaheen for four weeks.

He remembered his aunt's prickly comments when she'd read the letter. 'The press will be swarming all over the place, you mark my words. There'll be no more privacy! That girl attracts trouble, and it's just like Pavla to spring something like this on us.'

And now James was beginning to agree with her as he watched the gaggle of reporters and photographers vying with each other to take up their positions by the arrivals gate, each one hoping to be the first to glimpse the star of the biggest show to hit the television networks in a decade. And not to mention the steamy scandal between Leisal Adrian and Tony Sheraton, the show's director, providing the tabloids with all the juicy scandal they could ever wish for. The fact that her plane was late was giving them time to dig in, time to position themselves, to stake their claim to catch an off-guard indiscretion. But actors were always late, he considered unreasonably—it was a known fact—and this delay was probably a pre-arranged publicity stunt. The fact that it wasn't her fault she was stuck up in the air somewhere between here and London didn't really occur to him.

He sat down and looked at his watch again, stretching out his long legs. He was tall, over six foot, and his broad, powerful frame overshadowed everything around him. In all his thirty-four years—most of which he had spent in England—his education and his English way of life had done nothing to tame the wild, rebellious streak which flowed through his Irish veins, and his defiant nature fought constantly against any form of restraint. The strong, forceful thrusts of his hands dishevelled the dark crop of curly hair, as he ran his fingers through for the umpteenth time that morning.

He picked up the magazine from the table and looked once again at the exquisite face of the actress, smiling back at him from the glossy page. She was sitting cross-legged on a carved wooden bed, surrounded by rosy-pink satin cushions, and the picture was clearly staged to arouse any healthy red-blooded male. But as James examined the cream-coffee satin of her slip, and the velvet softness of her flesh, he found her beauty hard to define. Her delicate, high cheek-bones, thick tawny-red hair, and those enormous intelligent eyes set in a parchment-pale skin tantalized him easily enough. But beyond the surface beauty James saw something else. There was a mixture of pride and self-assurance, intermingled with a sensuality that was somehow untouched—somehow virginal.

He'd seen her last night on TV. It wasn't the kind of thing he would normally go out of his way to watch. These so-called blockbuster mini-series bored him to death as a rule—his taste leaned more towards the realities of life, to wildlife documentaries or political debates. But he'd deliberately forced himself to watch two hours of *Sister of Judaea* more out of curiosity than anything else, just to see what kind of girl was coming to Hanaheen, and what was so special about her that made everyone rave. And he'd had to admit he'd been impressed by Leisal Adrian's dramatic sincerity in the starring role—even if she did make an unlikely nun—and even more so by her breathtaking sexuality as she moved across the screen, in and out of the scenes.

'I wonder,' he mused. 'Are you real, Leisal Adrian, or are you a fake—a fabulous dream created by the media, or a woman who could love a man from the depths of her soul? One thing's for sure, it's going to be interesting to find out.'

His absorption in the actress was distracted when he heard the disembodied voice from the public-address system tell him that Flight 503 from London was at last arriving at gate six. He tossed the magazine carelessly onto the seat beside him and moved towards the group

4

of reporters.

* * *

Leisal Adrian gave it a couple of minutes before she moved from her seat in the aircraft, turning up her collar as she looked out of the window at the driving rain. She felt completely depleted, drained, and irritable and she couldn't wait to get out of the claustrophobic atmosphere of the aircraft and into the fresh air.

It had been an awful flight. The turbulence at times had scared her to death, although as a rule she loved to fly, and the fat, gold-ringed businessman occupying the seat next to hers was lucky he hadn't had his face slapped long before now. She'd felt his piggy eyes mentally undressing her at least a hundred times since take-off, and when the plane touched down she knew he'd been waiting for her to move first, just to be able to feel her legs against him as she squeezed past. It was nothing new. She was used to men looking at her in that way and she had grown adept at handling the worst of them.

He stood up at last, reaching for the hand baggage above his head, and Leisal heaved a sigh of relief. She had looked forward to this holiday for weeks. If anyone had told her five years ago that she would feel that she never wanted to see a camera again, she would have thought they were mad. *Sister of Judaea* had been the last straw, the tension and the squabbles between them all—the actors, the directors, and the crew—all of them without exception; and then the final hostile row with Tony. As her director he had been perfect, bringing out the depths of her character as only he could do, and he had made the show a smash-hit. But as a lover ...! And the one thing that made it all so much worse was that she'd believed him to be her friend. She shivered. Leisal didn't even want to think about it any more, it had been an awful time, and now, if only the newspapers would leave her alone to get on with her life, it was over, thank God. Four weeks of utter peace and tranquillity lay waiting for her here. Here there was none of the emotional hype—no rat race—or so Boushka had promised. 'Stay with my old friend—I'll write to her. She will help you find a little peace.'

Leisal turned her head towards the window again and her heart sank as she saw the group of reporters waiting by the gate like a pack of hunting dogs. Tony had promised her that no one would know of her whereabouts: he had given his solemn oath that she could take this holiday in complete anonymity—he'd even told her he'd booked her seat under an assumed name so that she could travel alone. Tony's promises were like brittle glass—broken in a moment if he could make publicity out of her, or more money.

The passengers, their heads bent against the galeforce wind, straggled their way across the tarmac, and James's eyes scanned each one until, at last, he saw her stepping from the aircraft. His intelligent eyes recognized her at once, and he couldn't help but give a flicker of a smile at the huge pair of tinted glasses hiding her eyes, and the square of brightly coloured silk which barely covered the unmistakable tawny redness of her hair. If that was supposed to be some kind of disguise it was doomed to failure before it got off the ground. Even if she'd put her head in a bin bag there would be no mistaking those terrific legs. But she moved down the steps of the plane with an air of assurance, an authority, and he saw her take off the glasses and thrust them into the pocket of her raincoat, hitching up the collar against the wind and disappearing quickly through the gate.

Suddenly, there she was, a lovely, long-legged woman in her mid-twenties, standing less than three yards away from him. He made his way forward, but, before he could reach her, she was overwhelmed by the reporters as they crowded in, and the sound of cameras clicked and whirred above the clamour of their voices. All at once it had become like bedlam. People were running towards her from all direction, some brandishing magazines or notebooks, even scraps of paper, anything that was at hand, just so long as she would sign her autograph for them; and for a few stunned seconds James looked on the madness in complete bewilderment. Then, in a couple of determined strides, he stepped forward and jostled his way through the crowd, pushing his broad shoulders unceremoniously against the newsmen and autograph hunters until, in a matter of seconds, he was by her side, with his arm firmly placed around her slim back, drawing her slowly but surely through the crowds.

'Miss Adrian?'

Startled, and very much on her guard, Leisal looked up into his face. 'Yes ...?' Her voice was low and well modulated.

James saw at once that her beauty was even more startling than the cameras could ever reveal. Her hair, under the silk scarf, was long and thickly curled, almost the colour of copper, with subtle shades of amber lighting its depths, her wide-spaced hazel eyes and creamy skin gave her a gentle, vulnerable, yet touch-me-not look that James found irresistible. She was stunning and he wished she would say something and switch off the batteries of those unbelievable eyes.

'I'm James Lovell—Harriet Lovell's nephew. I'm here to take you to Hanaheen. My car is over there. Are you ready? We'd better make a run for it.'

'Miss Adrian—what have you to say about

your affair with Tony Sheraton?'

'Will Sheraton be joining you . . . ?'

'Are you making another series, Miss Adrian . . . ?'

'Miss Adrian! One more picture please.'

'Who is that with you?'

'Miss Adrian . . . smile, please!'

The reporters were relentless in their pursuit of the actress and James angrily snatched the two pieces of luggage from the bewildered porter, thrusting the smaller one under his arm and grabbing up the other; then taking hold of Leisal with his free hand, he roughly elbowed his way through the hurly-burly of the crowds and steered her towards the doors until, at last, they were free from the clutches of the yelling mob and out into the daylight. They sprinted across the car-park, dodging the more persistent reporters and cameramen until they reached his car.

Once inside and settled in her seat, Leisal took off the dripping scarf and shook the tangled mass of her hair, then sat back with a sigh, closing her eyes momentarily as if to shut out the pandemonium that had assaulted their senses. James hurriedly threw her cases into the boot and climbed in beside her, giving her a wry look as he started the engine and, in a screech of tyres, accelerated away. Leisal had been quick to spot his cursory glance at the curve of her thighs and she pulled her legs more tightly under the seat as a reflex action but strangely, this time, there was no familiar rise of her hackles, this time there was no hint of the wolfish lust she had become accustomed to. Instead, his glance was purely the attraction of a normal, healthy male to a normal, healthy female and she felt oddly flattered by his obvious admiration.

'Is it always like this?' he asked, as the car raced towards the gates.

Leisal turned her head to the man beside her, examining his profile as he steered the car out of the crowded car-park and on to the road. His dark hair was rumpled and wet and his eyes betrayed an indefinable wariness. She found herself wondering what kind of man he was and why she could feel him striking an invisible, responsive chord somewhere deep inside her. 'I'm afraid so. I'm sorry you were caught up in the madness, no one was supposed to know I was here except your aunt,' she replied with the ghost of a smile.

'The whole of Ireland knows you're here— who's kidding who?'

She glanced quickly at his bemused profile, 'So it would seem,' she agreed quietly. 'But I assure you, none of it was my idea.'

'They must be raving lunatics.'

She held up a hand as if to silence him. 'Don't.' Her voice was almost a whisper. 'Please, I've waited for this holiday for a long time, I'd like to forget about all that kind of thing—I want to get away from the madness and enjoy some peace and silence for a while.'

James shook his head and concentrated on the road. They had left the airport and the town far behind them now, as James headed south towards the mountains and the mouth of Bantry Bay. Hanaheen, James's home, lay in splendid isolation just a few miles from the most south-westerly point of Ireland, and the scenery was giving way to rocky cliffs and wild moorland, while in the distance Leisal could see the blurred, grey outline of the mountains. It was a harsh and uncompromising terrain and reminded her of the wild moors of Yorkshire where she'd once spent an unforgettable holiday as a child.

Looking out of the window, she could see the coastline now and the breakers of the ocean pounding relentlessly against the shore below them, yet the further south they went, the more the sky began to lighten and the rain, stopping for the moment, allowed the sun to show a watery face through the heavy mass of cloud. It couldn't last long, though. She could see the grey clouds still hanging low in the sky and threatening more heavy weather yet to come.

She turned her head to James. 'I didn't know Harriet Lovell had a nephew—Boushka didn't tell me of you.'

'Boushka?'

'My grandmother.'

He laughed, and when he spoke again

11

Leisal detected the hint of an Irish brogue, 'Boushka! I've never heard anyone give their granny a name like that before. Why on earth do you call her that? What's wrong with "grandma" or "granny"?'

Leisal smiled. 'It's a term of endearment—it's a form of Russian.'

'Like Leisal? Is that where Leisal comes from—your Russian background? It sounds more German to me, or is that your stage-name and you're really called something quite normal like Mary or Kathleen?'

'No, Leisal's my real name, and yes, it's either Russian or German.' She threw him a teasing, side-long glance. 'My full name's Leisal Pavlova Leontina Adrianovitch.'

'Good Lord! That's quite a mouthful.' James chuckled, then he glanced across at her briefly as he added, 'Sorry, I didn't mean that to sound rude.'

'It's all right, I'm used to it, and I agree, it *is* a bit of a mouthful.'

Leisal glanced again at the man by her side. The amused expression had completely transformed his face and she turned away quickly to look out of the window as she felt an imperceptible quickening of her heartbeat.

'Leisal . . .' He said her name again quietly.

'Yes?'

'Oh, nothing, I was just thinking. Leisal—It has a nice ring to it. Are you called after your mother? Was—is she an actress too?'

12

'No, she was a dancer.'

'Was? Is she retired now?'

'She died a long time ago, when I was little.'

'Oh, I'm sorry, I didn't know.'

'That's alright, I hardly remember her, my grandmother brought me up, she even gave me her name.'

'Boushka?'

'Of course not,' she smiled. 'Adrianovitch. So you see, the stage is in our blood. I believe Leisal comes from someone in my grandmother's family—her sister I think. Boushka was an actress once, quite a famous one—you may have heard of her. Pavla Adrian?'

James shook his head. 'I've heard her name mentioned at home but I didn't know she was a famous actress.'

'Boushka tells me that was how she met your aunt, when she was on the stage—is your aunt an actress too?'

'Good Lord, no! But she remembers your granny well enough—Harry did say something about knowing Pavla Adrian when they were young.'

'Harry?'

'That's what I call my aunt. And by the way, I ought to warn you, she's got this thing about actresses—thinks they're all predatory creatures.'

'Well, thanks for the warning. I'll try not to take a bite out of you.'

He laughed. 'I wouldn't mind at all if you did.'

They drove on along the deserted road, not passing another living thing, either human or animal, until finally James slowed the car and pulled as near to the verge of the road as he could.

'Feel like some air?' He smiled gently, his attractive eyes sweeping her face. 'You're looking a bit pale.'

She returned his smile and nodded as he turned the car off the road and drove slowly along a narrow lane, stopping on the edge of the sheer cliffs. The lane ahead of them spiralled tortuously towards the white strip of beach, and looking down, Leisal felt a little giddy, as her eyes followed its winding course around the cliffs until it reached the sea. They were perched between the cleft of two high crags, several yards from the main road, and well out of sight of anyone who happened to pass by. It was so desolate a place that she could easily believe there was no one else left in the world.

Leisal gazed out over the swirling sea below them, strangely excited by the wildness of the spectacular seascape. She felt James's slight movement. He straightened up, resting an arm lightly on the wheel and stretching the other along the back of her seat, his hand brushing her hair and then dropping lightly onto her shoulder. Leisal was struck again by the man's extraordinary good looks, and the hypnotic depths of his eyes as they smiled into hers, like a steady flame shining out from the blackness.

'This is a local beauty spot,' he said, taking his hand off the wheel and making a circular movement. 'In summer it's packed with tourists.' He pointed towards a small island lying just visible across the bay and the two high, craggy rocks that dominated it. 'See those rocks out there, standing by themselves?' Leisal nodded as he went on to explain. 'They call them "The Sand Dancers" and it's easy to see why, isn't it?'

Leisal looked up at the rocks. 'I suppose so ... they do look as though they're doing some kind of crazy dance.'

'Aren't they fantastic? I've been intrigued by them since I was a kid. By the way, I saw you on TV last night.'

Leisal looked back at him in sharp surprise. He didn't look the type who would sit in front of the television watching something as romantic as *Sister of Judaea*. 'Did you?' she asked, with a small smile. 'What did you think about it?'

'It was all right—and you were pretty good—but I prefer to look at something like those dancers out there. They're real.'

Leisal gave a surprised laugh at his directness. 'And you feel I'm not?'

He smiled, but made no comment, so she looked out again at the two rocks. It was

15

clearly evident how the towering cliffs got their name. Their shapes, outlined starkly against the sky, had been fashioned for centuries by the harsh elements gusting in from the Atlantic, until now they resembled two towering humans, a man and a woman, two wild dancers on the edge of the world: one, with arms uplifted, reaching for the sky; the other frozen in a pirouette, its granite skirts clinging tightly to the gaunt shape of its torso. The Dancers were impressive, there was no doubt about it, and Leisal could see why this was a popular spot with tourists. Yet as she looked at the two giant rock dancers she felt a chill deep inside her. She didn't like them very much. They looked far too frightening, almost menacing.

She turned her eyes away from them as James got out of the car and came round to open her door. 'Come on, let's take a breather, we've another hour's drive before we get to Hanaheen.'

Leisal followed him slowly down the steep path between the cliffs, until their feet sank into the soft sand of the beach below. The rain had stopped but the wind was still blustering like a living thing, snatching at anything that lay in its path, and the breakers thundered up against the craggy rocks of the coastline, as though playing a mischievous game of hide-and-seek.

There was no sign of habitation for miles,

the only sign of humanity being the marks of the tyres from James's car on the track above. They started down the beach, the wind threatening to take her breath away, and yet filling her with a surge of exhilaration. There was a glorious feeling of wildness and freedom, and as she walked by James's side, his tall frame protecting her from the wind from the sea, she slowly felt the hard knots of tension begin to fade. They walked on for a good five minutes until James stopped at the bottom of one of the high, towering rocks and indicated with his hand for her to sit beside him on a ledge which was sheltered from the wind.

'This must make quite a change from the Holy Land,' he said, once they were seated.

She laughed, a light, merry sound. 'I wouldn't know: I've never been there.'

He threw her a quick glance. 'But I thought *Sister of Judaea* was set in the Holy Land?'

'So it was,' Leisal laughed again. 'But we did most of the location shots in the Brecon Beacons. It was freezing, too, believe me. The nearest any of us got to Jerusalem was the occasional artichoke in a restaurant in Abergavenny.'

'Was that where it was filmed: Wales?' James gave a low whistle, as Leisal nodded her head. 'Well, who'd have believed it, you live and learn.' His eyes were intent, taking in every inch of her face. 'How can you stand the

17

kind of life you lead?'

Leisal shrugged. 'It's the life I've chosen, and it has its compensations.'

The wind whirled around their legs but Leisal was content enough in the solitude of the cove.

'Warm enough?' James asked.

She snuggled further against the ledge. 'Quite warm enough.'

'It's a crazy life you lead, isn't it?'

'Some people might think so; but I've told you: it has its compensations.'

'What compensations?'

Her voice was barely audible above the sound of the wind. 'I happen to love it. I don't know anything else.'

'But what if you meet someone and want to get married. Would you leave the stage?'

Leisal laughed and made a small gesture of dismissal with her hand. 'You don't believe in beating about the bush do you? This is worse than an audition.'

'But would you?'

'I don't intend to get married,' she said carelessly. 'I don't think I could live with an actor's ego.' James noticed a small frown momentarily cross her brows betraying painful memories as they crept back into her mind. 'Or marry anyone connected with the stage.'

'Why should it be an actor?'

'All the men I know are in the business.'

'It's just possible you may meet someone

who isn't. What would happen then?' James's tone was genuinely curious.

'I've never really met anyone who's not in the business, so the question doesn't arise.'

'You've met me.'

Leisal's eyes cooled. 'That's different.'

James smiled and Leisal noticed again that disarming, attractive smile as his dark eyes held hers for the briefest of moments. 'I can't see why it's different. There must be someone, somewhere, who could make you change your mind.'

His words were said jokingly, she knew that, but for some incomprehensible reason they pleased her, and she was acutely aware of an odd, sharp tingle somewhere in the pit of her stomach. She decided to change the subject quickly. 'What about you?'

'Me? What about me?'

'What do you do?'

'I breed horses.'

Leisal waited for him to tell her more about himself, but as the seconds ticked by and he said nothing, she went on. 'Oh yes, that's right, I remember now. Hanaheen is famous for its racing thoroughbreds, isn't it? I remember Boushka saying something about it now. Does that take up all of your time?'

'Not all of it, I paint as well.'

'Paint what?' He shrugged, as though reluctant to answer, so she prodded jokingly. 'Houses? Toenails?'

19

The corners of his eyes crinkled as he grinned. 'Pictures. I paint pictures, landscapes, seascapes, sometimes portraits—but I'm not very good at that. That is why I love it here: it has everything. I love to be somewhere like this and try to put what I feel on canvas. I've loved painting for as long as I can remember. It relaxes me.' He turned quickly to face her almost as though he was embarrassed to admit his love for art. 'Are you sure you're warm enough?' he asked.

'I'm fine.'

His eyes were all over her and, meeting his gaze, she read an odd mixture there. Curiosity? Admiration? A little contempt perhaps?

'Been to Ireland before?' he asked.

She shook her head. 'Never.'

'The month of March isn't exactly the best time to come—I would have thought you'd have chosen somewhere more exotic for your holiday.'

Leisal laughed a little derisively. 'Ireland's perfect. It's remote—isolated. And that's exactly what I need right now, complete isolation. I need to get away from people whose values have got lost somehow.'

There was a brief pause and Leisal was aware of his sideways glance.

'What a life you must lead, when you can't trust anyone.'

'It's not quite as bad as that,' she answered

20

quickly.

She untied the scarf from her head and her hair tumbled about her face, heavy like a bright shower of rain and it reminded James, even in the dark shadow of the cliff, of the soft light of a candle's glow.

'Why do you do it?'

Leisal looked up at him in quick surprise. 'Do what?'

'Act. Why do you act? It always seems such an artificial life, making believe, playing games in front of a lot of people who have nothing better to do.'

She gave a small, surprised laugh. 'I don't think of it as that.'

'But that's what it is, isn't it? Nothing's real about it.'

'I could say the same thing about you. Why do you paint?'

'That's different.'

'No, it isn't. You've pretty well admitted that you paint because you love it very much. Why do you paint?'

He gave a small shrug of his shoulders as he let his eyes wander over to the horizon of the grey sea. Leisal, wanting to know more and more about this man by her side, asked, 'Do you sell pictures?'

This time James laughed: it obviously amused him to think that he could make money out of his pictures. 'I wish I *could* make my living at it, but I don't.' There was another

21

pause of just a few seconds then he said, quietly, 'I make my money from my stud and the farm, and a little from my gallery in London; that, and a few other things . . .'

'What other things?'

There was another slight pause then when he spoke again his voice was quiet and deliberate. 'Oh, a few business interests I inherited from my family.'

Leisal had the feeling that it was only a half-truth, but she didn't press him for more. They sat together, silent, watching the sea throw itself against the shore, listening to the shrill cry of the gulls as they soared above their heads. Presently, James stirred and said, 'Come on. We'd better make a move, it'll be dark in an hour.'

He took her very gently by the elbow and together they walked back across the sand towards the car. She glanced quickly at James as he unlocked the door for her. The fading daylight had blurred the sharpness of his profile but, even so, Leisal noticed that the dramatic slant of his dark lashes cast a sharp contrast across the angle of his cheek-bone. He looked tense and thoughtful as he stood, head bent, slotting the key in the door of the car.

She turned her face towards the sea, concentrating her thoughts on the choppy water and watching it heave sullenly below them. They drove on in silence as the last vestiges of the reluctant sun finally disappeared over the grey horizon. Apart from the still-light sky, the only brightness for miles came from the headlights of the car. It was almost seven-thirty when they turned into the gates of Hanaheen.

CHAPTER TWO

'Well, here we are. Home, sweet home!' James, his good humour apparent, carried her bags into the hallway of the house and Leisal caught her breath as she went through the heavy oak door. It had the look of another time, serene in its faded gentility, yet, as Leisal followed James along the hall that lead to a great winding staircase, she found herself suddenly grow cold. It wasn't the sort of physical cold that came from the knife-edged wind, or the jaded numbness that springs from travel-weariness. And it wasn't the stark pangs of hunger that made her shiver. It wasn't any of those. It was the dispiriting feeling one gets when something doesn't feel quite right, an uneasy feeling. Leisal didn't feel welcome, almost as though the house itself was telling her to go back from where she came.

'Bridget!' James opened a door at the bottom of the hall. 'Bridget! Our guest is here—will you stop what it is you're doing and

23

show her to her room, please?' Then he turned that strikingly attractive smile back to Leisal. 'Dinner in an hour. I'll take your bags up and see if I can find Harry. I'm surprised she isn't here. It isn't like her to go missing when we have someone to stay.'

Within a few moments Leisal was being shown to her room by an elderly housekeeper who wheezed her way up the stairs and opened a door at the end of a long gallery. James followed them and put her bags down inside the door, then giving Leisal a cheerful wink he strode off back down the stairs to look for his aunt. Bridget turned down the bed and showed her the bathroom, informing Leisal of the routine of the house in her rich Irish brogue. When she had gone, Leisal showered and, wrapping herself in a white bath towel, opened her case and rummaged among the dresses and underclothes until she found what she was looking for, a pair of silk trousers with a matching loose top. When she was dressed and ready to go downstairs again she sank into a chair and closed her eyes for a moment, finding herself once again wondering at the responsive chord James Lovell awoke in her.

She shrugged impatiently and got up, moving to the window and lifting the heavy velvet curtains to one side to look out along the side of the house. The sky was pitch-black but in the dim lighting of the courtyard she could see that the house was old-fashioned, grey-stoned and gabled, and the front façade was almost completely concealed beneath a thick canopy of ivy. Its upper storey was turreted above the trees, quite exposed to the weather from the sea and the mountains, while the lower half rambled outwards towards a glass conservatory.

Leisal shivered as she closed the window and glanced at her watch. Lord, she was hungry. She picked up her bag and made her way down the stairs trying desperately to shrug off the uneasy feeling which had settled upon her since she arrived. When she reached the bottom stair James's voice broke through her morbid preoccupation.

'I hope you found everything you needed in your room.'

She swallowed hard as she murmured her appreciation of the luxurious room the Lovells had provided for her stay at Hanaheen, willing her depressing thoughts away, as she felt the touch of his hand on her arm. He led her into the dining room.

'I expect you'll be glad of a bite to eat. Ah! here's Harry with the welcome-mat.'

Even as he spoke, the conservatory door leading from the dining-room opened, and, in the shaft of light, Leisal could see the silhouette of a tiny, fragile-looking woman standing in the doorway. James took Leisal's hand and led her towards the tiny figure and, in the brief silence that followed the old lady's arrival into the room, Leisal heard the solemn ticking of an old grandfather clock standing in the corner and she felt again that strange feeling of the past, as though she were stepping back in time.

'Harry, may I present the famous Leisal Adrian; and what's more she's starving—will dinner be long?'

Leisal had been aware of Harriet Lovell's eyes watching her closely and she met the woman's gaze squarely. The woman, like the house, seemed frozen in time, and Leisal's experienced eye could tell at a glance that the delicate, lavender-coloured twin-set above the tweed skirt must have cost more than three times the amount of her own silk suit. She also noticed the enormous sapphire ring glinting on the woman's bony left hand.

In the fleeting moments that the two women stood sizing each other up, Leisal could see that the old lady had a quiet air about her and that once she must have been very beautiful. Yet she looked so delicate and fragile that a puff of wind might blow her away. Her white hair was soft but thick, and coiled high on her head. And her face, although finely lined, was creamy and pink, and reminded Leisal of a faded peach.

Leisal moved towards the woman instinctively, her hand already outstretched in anticipation of James's introduction, but she hesitated momentarily and her hand wavered

26

as she saw the cold glint of hostility in the old grey eyes. The woman put out a soft, well-manicured hand but as Leisal grasped it she could feel no warmth. Harriet Lovell's smile was polite and courteous but, again, there was no sign of genuine welcome as her gaze swept Leisal from head to foot.

'How is your grandmother?' Her voice was soft, dry, and entirely without cordiality.

'Boushka is well and sends her love.'

'You are very pretty, my dear: almost as pretty as everyone says you are.'

'Thank you, and it's kind of you to let me stay here. I've been looking forward to coming to Hanaheen—Boushka's told me a great deal about you.'

The fine eyebrows arched and Leisal tried to tell herself that she was imagining the coldness of the woman, and that there was no hostility in the grey eyes. But then, if Leisal had any doubts about her welcome, they were confirmed now by the tenderness with which Harriet Lovell greeted the appearance of the slim dark-haired girl who came through the door of the dining-room.

The old lady clasped the girl warmly, hugging her as though she were a long-lost child. With a graceful movement, the girl at last broke away from Harriet's embrace and moved across to greet them.

She was a beauty. The darkness of her hair enhanced the slate-grey of her expressive eyes,

27

as did the delicate tone of her skin. 'James, darling.' The girl's voice was low and sensual and she threw her arms around James's neck and kissed him. 'Sorry I missed you this morning.'

'Enid,' James drew Leisal towards him. 'I'd like you to meet Leisal Adrian.'

'Well, of course,' laughed Enid, with a swift scrutiny that took in Leisal from head to toe. 'Hello, Leisal. I hope you don't think I'm going to be friends with you—you're far too attractive to be left alone with James. I should hate to think you would steal him from me.'

The girl's remark was made with such good humour that Leisal knew it wasn't to be taken seriously; so she laughed with her and said, 'Hello, Enid.' Then, as she felt Harriet Lovell's eyes staring coldly into the back of her head, she added, 'Don't worry, I never eat men on holiday: it ruins the digestion.'

'I'm relieved to hear it,' James laughed. 'Come on, let's have a sherry before we eat.'

They moved into a small pleasant room adjacent to the dining-room and Leisal looked around at the pleasing elegance of the chintz-covered chairs and the old marble fireplace that went so well with the feeling of bygone days. They sat before a glowing log fire, James comfortably lounging on the sofa and Enid perched on the arm, her hand resting lightly on his shoulder.

Harriet Lovell moved stiffly to sit herself in

28

an old high-backed chair by the fire and it was all so very ordinary and so very civilized that Leisal began to feel that perhaps her bad feelings for the place had been mistaken and that she had over-reacted because of the long, tiring journey.

She sat herself down on the edge of a chair as Harriet spoke to Enid.

'You will stay to dinner, Enid, won't you?'

'Of course, Harry, I haven't seen James all day so I've saved myself for him this evening.'

Harriet's manner towards Enid was friendly and warm, quite different from the tone she used with Leisal. 'Now that you're engaged to my nephew you must spend more of your time here—we have plans to make for your wedding. You must look on Hanaheen as your home now.'

At the old lady's words Enid got up from her perch on the sofa with a laugh. 'I've always looked on it as my home, Harry.' Then, to James, ruffling his dark head: 'James darling, come with me will you? Mike's been asking to see you, one of the horses has gone lame.' She turned her dark head to Leisal. 'You will excuse us for a moment?'

'Of course.'

James heaved his long frame out of his seat and followed Enid out of the room. When they had gone Harriet turned a pair of blue frosty eyes to Leisal. 'Such a *nice*, *sensible*, girl.'

Leisal was desperately trying to disguise her

unreasoning disappointment behind a broad smile on hearing of James's and Enid's impending marriage. Why she should feel so depressed at the news of James's engagement she couldn't imagine, and she concentrated her thoughts on the old lady's words coming from across the room. As she listened, Leisal detected a note of wistfulness in the dry voice. 'I'm so glad she's marrying James. I've always looked on her as the daughter I've never had.'

Dinner was a formal, desultory affair, and Leisal, in spite of her ravenous hunger, couldn't do justice to the delicious roast-beef, or appreciate the heady sweetness of the superb wine. Not once throughout the meal did James's aunt direct her conversation to Leisal and it was a great relief to her when it was over and Aunt Harry bade them good-night. It was later, much later, when Enid had gone home, and when Leisal and James were once more seated with their coffee in front of the fire that Leisal suddenly felt very tired.

'Is there any more coffee?' Leisal's question broke the brooding quiet of the room, her voice sounding flat and weary.

She saw him glance sharply. 'It's all finished, but I can get Bridget to make some more if you like.'

Leisal shook her head. 'No, never mind, it's much too late.'

She clasped her hands across her arms and looked again at James Lovell. He must have felt her eyes watching him because suddenly he looked up and held her gaze for a long moment. The silence of the room was broken only by the slow ticking of the clock and the crackle of the logs in the fireplace. Leisal gave herself a little shake. Her eyes felt strained and heavy-lidded as tiredness overtook her.

'You must treat Hanaheen as your home for the next few weeks,' he said gently. 'You must come and go as you wish.'

'Thanks—I'd like that,' she replied softly. 'I need some time to breathe.'

His eyes were watching her closely as she talked, watching so intently that she turned her head away again and looked down at her hands on her lap.

'When a love affair goes wrong, time to breathe is what one needs, isn't it?' he murmured quietly.

Leisal didn't look up. She kept her eyes downcast, as though in fascinated contemplation of her hands. She sensed that he saw far too much and when she did look at him some moments later he was smiling, but still searching, still watching.

'You obviously know how it feels.' Leisal deliberately kept her voice light, it was far too late in the evening for heart-searching confessions.

James laughed. He picked up his brandy glass and drained the last few drops. 'Not me! I'm free as a bird. Totally untouched by female hand and I intend to remain so.'

Leisal looked up in surprise. 'But you're engaged—how on earth can you say that you're as free as a bird when I was introduced to your fiancée only this evening?'

He laughed again, and then sat back in his chair, eyeing her with a mischievous grin playing around his attractive mouth. 'Harry has this idea that Enid and I would make a perfect couple. Everyone expects us to get married one day—everyone except Enid and I, that is. We've been thrown together since we were kids and neither of us has felt the need to put anyone straight. She helps with the horses and, sometimes, she helps me at my gallery in London—she's no mean artist herself. I suppose it's very likely that we'll end up getting married one day: I'm very fond of her. But if either one of us meets someone else, then the other would be the first to wish them luck.' He got up, placing his glass on the table by his side.

'It hardly seems fair that you should get engaged to her if you expect to meet someone else.'

James gave a deep-throated chuckle. 'I don't expect to, and I'm not looking for anyone else; but it happens all the time, doesn't it? Anyway, I'm keeping you up and you must be exhausted by now.'

'I'm quite resilient, but I won't be sorry to get to bed tonight, it's been a long day.'

32

'I thought you actors came awake at night?'

'Only when we've slept all day.'

He held out an arm to help her from the chair. His hand covered hers, gently pulling her up, and suddenly they were standing close to each other. His face had lost that tense hardness now, and was softened by the good food and wine. They stood together, gently smiling one to the other, his smile doing strange things to her emotions. So strange were these feelings that they startled her and she broke away quickly and turned towards the door, saying almost apologetically, 'Good-night, James.'

'I'll see you to your room.'

He led her up the staircase and along the wide landing, holding his arm lightly around her back with the easy assurance of a lover. Leisal liked his touch, but the intimate feeling of his presence strangely unnerved her.

When they reached her door they exchanged another smile, 'Good-night, Leisal Pavlova Leontina Adrianovitch. Sleep well and I'll see you in the morning.'

When James had gone, Leisal closed the door of her room quietly and stood leaning against it. It was nearly midnight and she went across to the window, opening it and breathing deeply. The rain had stopped and a freshening wind was blowing in from the sea. She stood for several minutes thinking of James, until at last she turned away and moved over to the bed. Her legs felt like jelly. She undressed quickly and snuggled down into the bedclothes.

The last thing she wanted was to feel attraction for anyone, yet here she was, alone on the remotest point of southern Ireland, and already beginning to shake at the thought of James Lovell's touch. And even as she turned in the soft silkiness of the sheets, her body was already wanting to know his.

A small frown creased her forehead. What would his strange aunt think if she could read her thoughts now? The old girl certainly made no secret of her disapproval. Oh, well, she'd just have to change the old girl's mind for her about actresses, wouldn't she? And with that decision, Leisal snuggled further down in the bed and willed herself to sleep.

Leisal slept late and was awakened next morning by the rattle of the tea-tray which Bridget placed on the table by her bed. She stretched her arms, feeling refreshed and rested after a good night's sleep, and she lay contentedly with a pleasurable feeling of looking forward to the prospect of a brand new day.

'Good morning, Bridget,' she smiled, as she got out of bed and slipped her saffron silk robe around her slim shoulders.

The old lady murmured her greeting as she poured the tea, and Leisal crossed over to the window, inhaling deeply the fresh salty tang of the air. 'What a lovely day. Thank goodness the rain's stopped.'

Outside, the sunshine was lighting the courtyard in a golden shimmer and the trees threw a dappled shadow across the lawns. She looked beyond the trees to the hazy contour of the horizon, with an excited feeling of a holiday just beginning.

But then, as her eyes moved across the breathtaking scenery, she spotted them at the gate. Immediately, her heart sank like a stone. There was no mistaking the gaggle of men with cameras already crowding around the tall gates of Hanaheen—reporters looked the same no matter where she was—and her secret holiday hide-away was no longer a secret.

'Oh, no!' she murmured. 'I don't believe it!'

'Miss Harriet's had an awful time with them this morning, miss,' Bridget muttered. 'They won't go. They say they want pictures of you on your holiday.'

Leisal moved into the shadow of the curtains and out of view of the reporters. It was pandemonium. She lifted the curtains apart just a slit and looked out again. She could see the tall figure of James at the gate angrily signalling for them to leave and the tiny frame of Harriet standing in the doorway. She quickly showered and dressed and, by the time she reached the hall, James was coming back through the door, his face hard as a rock, vividly expressing his intense irritation at the persistence of the men hanging around outside.

'I sincerely hope that lot don't hang around for the rest of your stay here,' he stormed angrily. 'I had plans to take you out today, but how can any sane person move with that pack of wolves following every step we take.'

'I'll give them an interview, then perhaps they'll leave us alone.'

James made an inarticulate sound and strode down the hall towards the sitting-room. Leisal made to follow, but the dry voice of Harriet Lovell stopped her just as she started to move away.

'Come into the dining-room, Leisal. Your breakfast was ready hours ago.'

The woman's tone was brusque and the implication obvious. Here we go, thought Leisal and followed the ramrod back, dressed in the inevitable tweeds, through into the dining-room.

'I'll ring for Bridget to bring in your breakfast.'

'Please don't bother. I had tea and biscuits in my room, and that's enough for me, thanks.'

The two women stood in awkward silence as Harriet Lovell gazed out of the window at the group of reporters. Then the old lady turned to face her and their eyes met; and it was in that moment that Leisal saw that she had an implacable enemy: one she would never be able to win over.

She drew a hard, long breath and clenched her hands tightly. 'I'm sorry my arrival has caused so much disruption, Miss Lovell, but I'm sure if I give them a short interview they will go away and you will be left in peace.'

'And if they don't?'

'Then I will go.'

Aunt Harry said grimly, 'That's fair enough, I suppose.' Then she eyed Leisal for a long moment, her cold, inimical glance causing Leisal to shiver as she added, spitefully, 'I hope you are right, but perhaps it would be better if you made other arrangements anyway. I really don't think it advisable that someone like you should take your holiday here. Enid and James have little time together as it is, and I certainly don't like the idea of him escorting you all over the place as he suggested he would this morning.'

'Perhaps we should leave that decision to James.' Leisal's tone was polite, but inside she was seething with anger at this tiny lady who was standing before her with her white head held high, and her narrow back as straight as a ramrod. 'I don't expect to be escorted around by anyone. I'm quite capable of finding my own amusement.'

'Then I'll arrange for the press to interview you this afternoon.'

'No', Leisal began, then added as courteously as she could, 'I think it would be better if I discussed this first with James and find out from him when the best time would be.'

The old lady drew herself up to her full height and stared angrily at Leisal for a moment, then she turned and left the room. When she had gone, Leisal let out a long sigh and flopped down on to a chair. She would have to be the world's biggest optimist if she thought she could ever get the old girl to like her. But why, she asked herself, why had she taken such a dislike to her? Boushka had assured her that she would be made most welcome by her old friend. Was it because she thought Leisal was some threat to her plans for James's marriage to Enid? Did their marriage mean so much to her?

She went out into the hall to look for James. The sooner the press were satisfied that there was nothing here to interest them, the sooner they would go away and leave her to her holiday. She reached the sitting-room to find the door was slightly ajar, and giving it a soft tap Leisal pushed it open. James was sitting by the telephone and as she entered he shot her a look from under his fine brows, and when she spoke he heard a tight-sounding tone.

'Your aunt is quite upset by the press— would you mind if I arranged an interview? Perhaps they will go away then.'

His voice took on a hard, unpleasant undertone. 'They'd better,' he said shortly. 'The press are the last people I want hanging around Hanaheen. Not only is it very disturbing to my aunt, *I* don't want them here either.'

'Nor do I, and I apologize to you, as I have already done to your aunt. I don't know how they've found out I was here.'

'Well, they have!' He shot her another look. 'It's probably your boyfriend—and the filthy little scandal that's been entertaining everyone lately . . .'

Leisal stiffened, but her tone was mild as she interrupted: 'So you have already made up your mind about me—you and your aunt?'

His dark eyes scrutinized her from across the room. 'You're surely not going to deny all that's been said about you and Tony Sheraton, are you?'

Leisal sighed deeply. How could she deny anything? The press had made a meal of their affair, and no matter how many times she had tried to explain that it had all got out of hand, there was nothing she could say that made it better. She knew that it was far from a pretty story, and as she stood there listening to James Lovell's accusing voice, she could feel the anger wash through her bones and start up again the pain of the nightmare she had just come through. She could see again in her mind's eye the dark lines of strain etching across Tony's attractive mouth as she had said her final goodbye; and Leisal, looking now at the handsome figure of James Lovell standing before her with such dark accusation in his eyes, swallowed the bad feelings that were threatening to engulf her again. However, when she replied at last, her voice was calm and controlled. 'I don't have to explain to you—or to anyone for that matter, but as your guest I think I should at least spare you the embarrassment of all this. Perhaps if I gave you an explanation.'

'You don't have to explain—it's no concern of mine.'

'No, of course, you're quite right—it isn't. But it isn't quite how the press have made it sound.'

James shrugged. 'It never is, is it?'

Leisal sat down on a high-backed chair near the door and held his gaze squarely.

'I met Tony when we were rehearsing for *Sister of Judaea*. I'd heard of him of course, after all, who hasn't in my business?'

James's expression was almost baleful as she went on. 'We—we liked each other and got on like a house on fire. After a while we started going out a little, just a drink after rehearsals at first—that kind of thing—and before long the papers had us practically married.' James watched her as she sat quietly facing him: his eyes were wary, but he said nothing. Leisal went on. 'It was later, much later, when I found out he—'.

'I can guess.'

Angrily, Leisal retorted, 'How can you guess

40

anything? What can you possibly know of any of it?'

'I can read.'

'Yes. You can read like millions of others. You read of an empty-headed glamour-puss called Leisal Adrian running off with a married man! How cruel the press can be at times!'

'Are you telling me that it isn't true?'

Leisal took a deep breath. 'No, I'm not saying that. It is true . . . partly. But what the press didn't say was that when I found out about . . . about . . .'—her words dropped to almost a whisper—'*Suzanne*, I left him at once and went back home.'

James laughed: there was no mistaking the irony in the sound. 'Oh, my Lord! Are you saying that this man deceived you? Do you really expect me to believe that?'

'He *did* deceive me. I truly didn't know of his wife, let alone the fact that she was—ill.'

'*Ill!* What an understatement! A woman who's been in a coma since God knows when—and as a result of his drunken driving—and you—pretty innocent Leisal—not knowing *that*? Come off it, you'll have me believing in Father Christmas next.'

'I didn't know! *Truly!* I didn't!'

James stood up and looked down at her grimly, then he shrugged disinterestedly. 'Well, as I said, it's really no concern of mine, but the fact that we're all going to be hounded by newsmen while you're here, then that fact alone makes it a concern of mine. We'll arrange a press conference right now and perhaps we can all have some peace.'

He turned away abruptly. And there was something about his movement that stirred her. Something in his eyes had caused her heart to leap. He was impressive. Suddenly she wanted more than anything to please him.

This was ridiculous! She had been so badly hurt before that she had vowed no man would affect her again. She had come here to lick her wounds and yet here she was again, just two days into knowing James Lovell; playing games with herself, wanting him so much to like her, and jumping like a rabbit every time he looked at her. 'You must believe me, James.'

At the door he turned back, his expression less angry and his eyes revealing a more sympathetic expression. He held out his hand. 'Come on my poor little misunderstood Russian snow princess, let's get this press conference over with and then perhaps I can show you the real beauty of Hanaheen.'

Whatever his aunt thought of her, this man was not an enemy. The way he smiled into her eyes only made her like him more. She moved forward, taking his hand and smiling back at him. 'I can't wait to see Hanaheen.'

He led her from the room and into the hall. As they walked together, Leisal caught a glimpse of Harriet Lovell standing by the stairs. The old lady had the look of a cat that's just about to steal the cream, and Leisal's heart began to beat a warning.

CHAPTER THREE

Leisal stood thoughtfully at the window, watching the motorcade of press cars disappear through the gates of Hanaheen. All things considered it hadn't gone too badly. As usual, there had been the small cluster of over-keen reporters among them who had the trick of trying to trap her into saying things they wanted to hear, which they could twist around to make more colourful reading; but Leisal had grown almost as expert as they were at dodging the issue.

'You handled that well, Leisal,' was James's comment, when the last of the reporters had gone. 'Not bad at all. In fact, I'd go as far as to say you were quite fantastic.'

'Thank you,' smiled Leisal. For the first time in three hours James detected a hint of nervousness in her voice as she murmured, 'I only hope they keep their promise and stay away now as they said they would.'

'So do I.' James strolled across the room to stand by her side at the window. 'I was afraid you'd lose your nerve,' he said quietly, giving her a brief smile. 'And I wouldn't have blamed you if you had—I would have broken their nosy necks. Some of them really know how to go for the jugular, don't they?' He took her arm, turning her away from the window and leading her to the door, checking his watch as he did so. 'Anyway, it's over now and I don't know about you but I'm starving—fancy some lunch?'

'Mm . . . love some.'

'After that ordeal only the very best will do. Come on, I'll take you to Patten's in Drumcarrick: it's only down the road, a couple of miles from here—and Joe serves up the most fantastic steaks—real melt-in-the-mouth stuff.'

Leisal laughed. 'Sounds wonderful.'

'Besides, I want to show you off to the locals.'

Leisal looked at him with a startled laugh. 'Show me off?'

'Yes. Don't tell me you're shy, I thought actresses liked being shown off, and it's not often we have a celebrity to share our humble hostelry. Besides, I want to make every man in the place jealous of me, and I want to watch their wives eat their hearts out with envy.'

Leisal laughed again. 'Heaven forbid! And I think you underestimate actresses—well, this one certainly—almost as much as you underestimate women.'

'Why should I? It's a known fact that women resent other women who are more

44

attractive than themselves.'

'Do you believe that? I think it rather depends on the woman.'

James looked at her in astonishment, surprised by the question. 'Hell, I don't know, do I? It's what I've always believed.'

'Well, let me beg to differ on that one. Most women know their men well enough, probably more than they realize.'

'Come on, let's eat.' His tone was now matter-of-fact. 'I'm too hungry to argue with you, but first, I think it might be better if you changed into something more, er—practical.' His eyes were moving approvingly over her silk shirt, and lingering momentarily at the hint of cleavage exposed by the two top buttons casually left undone, and on the way the soft silky material emphasized her soft curves. 'Something warmer?'

'Something warmer? What on earth for? Where are you taking me for lunch—Siberia?'

He laughed, tucking her arm into his as they went out into the hall. 'The wind's quite cold, go and choose something warm and comfortable . . . and stop asking questions.'

He waited while she went back up to her room and changed into a pair of jeans and a sweater. When she rejoined him in the hall they went outside into the courtyard.

She was just about to step into the car when the thin sound of Harriet Lovell's voice reached them from the doorway. 'James!

Where are you going?'

'For a spot of lunch, won't be long.'

'Oh, but you can't—I've arranged for Lionel to come over to look at the mare.'

James turned to face his aunt. 'You needn't have bothered, Harry, there's nothing wrong with her—it was only a stone in her hoof. Mike and I got it out last night—she's fine.'

'I want Lionel to check her over all the same, you'd better stay here.'

'Mike can handle it.'

'I said, I want you to stay here.'

There was a note in his aunt's voice which caused James to tighten his lips and when he spoke again his voice sounded brittle and more than a little tense. 'And *I* said Mike could handle it.'

Leisal stood silent and thoughtful throughout the long moments of the battle of wills between James and his aunt. She knew this fuss about the mare was just an excuse. There was no disguising the angry glare Harriet Lovell was throwing her and she was left in no doubt that the old lady was trying to prevent him from taking her out to lunch.

She pretended to watch the fat goldfish as they swam lazily in the lily-padded pond in the courtyard, but her eyes were guarded as she caught James's eye. 'Forget it, James,' she said softly. 'If it's going to cause problems we can always go some other time.'

She heard his quick intake of breath and

glanced up to see the look of irritation on his face. 'No, we're not going tomorrow—we're going today. There's absolutely no reason why Mike can't handle it—he doesn't need me and Harry knows it.' Then to his aunt: 'See you later, Harry.'

He opened the car door and Leisal climbed in. She knew the old lady was still glowering angrily at them from the doorway but she didn't look back. James switched on the engine and the car moved away soundlessly, out of the drive and towards the little town of Drumcarrick.

Sitting across the table in the dim lights of Patten's Bar, Leisal caught her breath at the extraordinary inner strength and sensuality which exuded from James Lovell. Everything about him was attractive, from the top of his dark curly head to his expensively booted feet. She felt his leg brush against hers under the table, but whether it was intended or not she wasn't sure. One thing she was sure of was that she liked the feel of him, and she was certainly enjoying his company.

The steak had been wonderful and everything that James had promised, and as she met his gaze she saw the teasing expression flickering in their dark depths, as he felt her eyes examining him.

'Do I pass?' His smile was gentle. Leisal turned away quickly realizing that her flush of embarrassment amused him. She heard the chuckle in his voice as he queried, 'Enjoy your lunch?'

She nodded and patted her stomach. 'Wonderful. Now I'm too full to move.'

Their eyes met again across the table, and Leisal sensed rather than saw James's long and curious scrutiny, then he gave an odd little sigh and said so quietly that she almost didn't hear him, 'I'm glad you're here, Leisal.'

There was something in his tone which made her look away quickly. His words pleased her and she didn't want him to see the sparkle of pleasure which sprang into her eyes at his remark. Suddenly, and without warning, she felt an inner uneasiness as her guard went down for the briefest of moments. Leisal had always found public engagements easier to handle than intimate tête-à-têtes, especially with a man as attractive as James Lovell, so she looked around the room, pretending to be absorbed in the other occupants seated at the tables of the tiny restaurant. 'I wish your aunt felt the same,' she murmured quietly at last.

'What's that supposed to mean?'

'She resents my being here.'

Leisal turned her hazel eyes back to the attractive man facing her, and with a small shock she saw the look of incredulity in his dark eyes.

'Now, just a minute, that sounds too silly for words,' he protested. 'Where on earth did you get that idea?'

Leisal felt unable to hold back the words now and they came tumbling out: 'Perhaps it *is* silly, but I can't help feeling that she doesn't like me at all—as if I'm some sort of—oh, I don't know—some sort of nymphomaniac who'll steal you away—a threat to her plans for you and Enid.'

James grinned a little at that and reached for his wine. 'Leisal, simmer down, you've got it all wrong.'

Leisal gave a bitter exclamation: 'I don't think I have.'

James looked closely at her over the top of his glass. He lifted it to his mouth and drained the last drop of wine then said, grimly, 'I agree she can sound bossy and sharp-tongued sometimes, but remember, she's an old woman now. She's vain, a little prejudiced, and very possessive with her family, and she's set in her ways. She's had a free hand to run Hanaheen since my mother died and perhaps that makes her try to run people's lives for them—but in her mind it's all in their best interests.'

Leisal made an inarticulate sound and bit her tongue. She longed to tell him how much she would like to wring the old lady's neck but thought better of it. Instead she asked, 'Why did she never marry?'

He shrugged slightly and shook his head. 'I honestly don't know. She was quite a beauty when she was young. I believe there was someone once, but he went off and married someone else.' James gave a small sigh as he remembered the gossip, then looked across at Leisal with that teasing look back in his eyes. 'I seem to recall that he ran off with an actress. Perhaps you're right, perhaps she believes you will carry me off, eh? If you did, I wouldn't put up much of a struggle—quite the reverse as a matter of fact.' He chuckled softly. 'I can't think of a better fate—it's always been an ambition of mine to be abducted by a beautiful nympho.' He winked and his brow lifted as he waited for her reaction, but when Leisal made no comment he went no more thoughtfully, 'Seriously though, once you get to know her properly you'll love her, I know you will.'

Leisal bit back her reply, 'I shouldn't bet on it', and instead she kept quiet and finished her wine. James grinned again and beckoned the waiter then shot her a teasing, sidelong glance. 'We'd better get a move on or the afternoon will be over.'

'Where are we going?'

'Wait and see.'

They moved their way through the amiable crowd that had gathered in the bar, James laughing and chatting to his friends and introducing Leisal to Joe Patten, like a long-lost friend whom he had known all his life instead of just a couple of days.

'You'd better let me have your autograph, miss, or me wife'll never forgive me,' Joe grinned as he shook her hand. 'She never missed an episode of *Sister of Judaea*.'

'I'd be glad to. But better still, Joe, I've some photographs back at Hanaheen. I'll see that you get one before I leave.'

Back in the car and looking through the window, Leisal had to admit that the scenery around her was glorious. The late March sun had deepened the sky to a blood-red glow, and the trees bordering the narrow road spiked needle-sharp thrusts above the sleepy branched willows and hawthorns. Along the curve of the hillside she squinted her eyes to see a stately procession of riders silhouetted against the sky as they exercized a string of horses; and as she listened to James explaining the rigorous routines necessary to run a successful racing stable, she thought how perfect the setting was.

She observed his profile, as he talked now so easily, and she admired the strength of his hands on the wheel of the car, and without any warning another thought entered her mind. In the soft beauty of such a setting, how easy it would be to fall in love. It seemed impossible on this lovely afternoon that anyone could throw a shadow on its perfection but, nevertheless, the image of James's aunt flickered through her thoughts and she shivered inwardly.

The road descended sharply and James negotiated the car along a twisting deserted path. Here and there Leisal glimpsed small,

51

whitewashed cottages with their thatched roofs peeping through the hedgerows, and then some way ahead she saw the mirror-like sheen of an open stretch of water.

'Here we are.' James stopped the car along the banks of a lake and Leisal looked out on the vast expanse of water, misty and silent in the late afternoon sun. 'This place is a favourite haunt of mine.' She saw the brief flash of white teeth as he smiled at her and the glimmer of amusement in the dark eyes. 'Do you like it?'

Leisal nodded silently, her eyes wide as they stepped out of the car into the fresh coolness of the lakeside. The air was still and fragrant and again Leisal felt that strange feeling of timelessness as she breathed in the gentle air. James slipped his arm through hers and he pretended not to notice that she clutched his sleeve tightly as they walked along the shore.

Leisal glanced up into the sky and turned to smile at him. Her smile was so rare, so lovely, that for a brief second it took his breath away and caused him to smile, too, as she asked, 'Where are we?'

'Ballyhoe.'

'It's glorious,' she said, 'but I'm glad you had the brains to tell me to change, it's pretty wild out here.'

'Yes, it is. The lake is Ballyhoe—and don't ask me what it means in the Gaelic because I've no idea. Come on, I've a boat tied up along here, I thought we might do a spot of fishing.'

Leisal laughed. '*We*? I like the way you've decided that I might like to do a spot of fishing as you put it. Do you always make arrangements for people whether they want it or not?'

The look on his face was one of complete surprise. 'What's the matter? Don't you like to fish?'

'I don't know—I've never tried it before.'

'Then you don't know what you've missed.' He grabbed hold of her hand and led her along the shore of the lake. 'You'll love it.'

Leisal grinned, 'If you say so. But what about rods and things?'

'No problem.'

Almost as soon as he'd spoken, James led her to a small wooden cabin and opened the door with a key he had taken out of his pocket. Inside the cabin Leisal detected the faint aroma of fish and, once her eyes had become accustomed to the dimness, she could make out an assortment of rods, reels, hooks, and even bait. In fact, everything anyone would need for a few hours fishing on the lake. James stowed it all into the front end of the boat and then helped her clamber gingerly in, lifting a rope out of the water, to which a large piece of rock was attached to act as an anchor. He took the oars and rowed out towards the centre of Ballyhoe.

'You think of everything, don't you?' Leisal asked, when they had dropped the anchor again and James was baiting a line for her.

'I try to. Here, take this.' He handed her the line. 'And try not to get it tangled in the weeds, cast it over there, that spot looks promising.' He indicated with his finger a point on the lake. 'There should be plenty of roach just about there.'

'How can you know that? Did you send them a telegram to let them know that we were coming?'

'Very funny. Here, let me show you, you'll get all tangled up, holding it like that.'

The boat rocked precariously as James's long legs strode over the wooden slats of seats and stood behind her. It was a nice feeling having him stand so close, and Leisal felt the warmth of his powerful frame wrapping around her as his hands held hers to manipulate the thin line. There was a wonderful intimacy in their closeness, and if she had turned her head just a fraction his lips would have touched hers; and once again Leisal was made aware of James Lovell's powerful sensuality.

'Right, take the line back over your shoulder.' He ducked away as she lifted the rod, but his hands still held on to her at the waist, steadying her, 'OK, good. Now sit down and wait.' He moved back to the centre of the boat and concentrated on his own line, casting it out well away from hers.

She sat quietly content at her end of the boat, intrigued not so much by the intricacies of angling but by the fascinating contemplation of his profile—smiling a little as he reeled in a soggy clump of weeds.

'Damn weeds,' James swore. 'As fast as Mike cuts them away they grow back again like bloody triffids.' He cast out his line again and sat back meeting her gaze, then he smiled: that sudden, devastating smile that made Leisal's heart leap.

'This lake does strange thing to you if you're not careful,' he murmured.

'What sort of things?'

'It puts ideas into your head.'

There was a short silence. Leisal knew what he meant. Already she had had several ideas of what it would be like to make love to James Lovell, and her Aquarian Achilles' heel—that fear of intimacy—was weaving its gossamar web around her heart. The way to her protected heart was like crossing the Rubicon. 'I hardly think it's fair to blame the lake,' she smiled. 'If you're thinking what I think you're thinking, forget it.'

It was a shot at random but it went home and the dark eyes regarding her were suddenly full of amused challenge. 'Would it worry you?'

'Would what worry me?'

'Whatever it is I'm thinking—would it worry you?'

Leisal disguised her wariness beneath a broad smile. 'Whatever it is you're thinking, you can keep it where it belongs—in your thoughts. That way, it can't worry me at all.'

James shook his head thoughtfully. 'Don't bet on it.'

Leisal held his challenge and then turned away to look out over the lake. He was playing with her and she knew it. His words come again in a soft chuckle. 'I thought Russians were supposed to be passionate.'

At this, Leisal burst out laughing. 'You've been reading too much Chekhov.'

James smiled invitingly. 'I dreamed of you last night.'

'Really? That must have been exciting for you.' It wasn't the first time that line had been used on Leisal and it disappointed her. She would have thought that someone as intelligent as James Lovell could have come up with something better.

'Wasn't that a line from *Sister of Judaea*?' he parried.

'No, it wasn't and it's a line that's as corny as the jolly green giant.'

'I could've sworn I heard that wimp of a leading man say it to you just before that steamy love scene in the hold of the ship.' He grinned as she threw him a scornful glance. 'I remember the guy drooling over you: "I lay for hours",' he went on, his dark eyes teasing, ' "dreaming of you looking just like this—in a boat with me—alone ... imagining ... aching ..."' James held his arms towards her in a theatrical gesture. 'By the way, I've always wondered about something ...'

'What?'

'When two actors make love to each other on the screen like that, do they ...?'

'Well, go on, do they what?'

'Do they, you know, do they really feel sexy towards each other?'

Leisal threw back her head and burst out laughing. 'If you saw the hundreds of crew standing just yards away from you, watching every move, you'd soon be put off, believe me.'

'Well, that guy you were supposed to be in love with put on a good enough act, he looked as though he was enjoying every minute of his work.'

Leisal laughed again softly. 'I think Nigel fancied the second cameraman more than he fancied me.'

James arched his eyebrows in surprise and grinned. 'Oh well, you never can account for taste. Now if I'd been playing that part you'd have known you'd been made love to.'

'Come off it, James.' Then with an excited cry Leisal sat upright and pulled on the rod. 'Hang on, I think I've got a bite!'

Unfortunately, she hadn't. She'd caught nothing more exciting than a tangle of weeds and they spent another hour on the lake, but didn't catch a thing. A brisk wind had started up, blowing from the sea, and the rain-clouds gathering above them were so low and heavy that Leisal felt she could reach up and touch them. They packed up the tackle and made their way slowly back to the bank, mooring the boat to a narrow, creaky landing stage, before Leisal helped him unload the tackle and stow it back into the white-painted cabin. Everything had a place and it was in those few moments that Leisal learned something else about James Lovell. He was exceptionally tidy. He glanced up as Leisal struggled to lift one of the wicker baskets onto the shelf.

'Hang on, I'll lift that.' He took the basket out of her hand and threw it easily into its place, then he paused and turned abruptly to face her, standing so close that Leisal only had to lift her face to his. She was accustomed to men admiring her, used to recognizing their desire for her burning in their eyes. But nothing had prepared her for the way her heart reacted to James's searching look, and the way she wanted to feel his hands on her body, and the exquisite need to taste his mouth. He reached out and held her arms, then slowly, very slowly she felt herself being pulled into his arms. He hesitated for a brief moment, his dark eyes searching her, and then without haste he lightly touched her lips with his.

Suddenly she was in his arms and feeling the wonderful warmth of his body against hers.

James tightened his arms around her, aware only of the feel of her breasts pressed against his chest and of the softness and scent of her body. His lips were warm and full of tender passion, and they held each other in a loving embrace for long moments. She could feel his hands exploring her body and she thrilled as his touch sent spirals of deep-buried longing to awaken her. She wanted to stay in this man's arms forever.

Slowly, Leisal's brain began to clear and she suddenly pulled away, breaking herself free from his arms, frighteningly aware of the effect this man had on her emotions.

James's eyes opened and his arms fell to his side, breaking the embrace, and he stepped back unsteadily, murmuring softly, 'I'm sorry, Leisal, I didn't mean for that to happen.'

'Neither did I, James.' Leisal turned away abruptly, stooping to pick up a rod that was still lying by her feet. 'Let's just put it down to the magic of Ballyhoe.'

'I think it's something more than that.'

He took the rod from her hand and their fingers touched again. As she watched him stow the rod into a leather case it shocked her to realize the extent of her response to his touch, and she knew James was feeling the same. She wanted him to hold her again, to run his hands through her hair, to kiss her again and again.

He stepped back, concentrating on the last

item of tackle and placing it in its place on the shelf, then he turned and for a few moments they looked at each other. His eyes fell upon the gentle, uneven rise and fall of her breasts and it was clear to Leisal in those few moments that he had not expected to feel the way he did either. He took her hand and held it to his lips, saying in a low voice. 'If we don't get back now, Leisal, I believe I would keep you here forever.'

They walked back to the car in silence. She kept her eyes fixed on some spot ahead, aware of James's eyes looking down at her. He felt her shiver and drew his arm around her waist, but at his touch Leisal pulled away sharply, an instinctive movement that he tried not to notice, at first pulling her back and then letting her go, 'All right, I'm sorry.' His voice was light. 'I admit, I shouldn't have tried it on.'

'Then why did you?'

He stopped and turned her to face him, taking her hands in his. 'Even a saint would struggle to keep his hands to himself if he were alone with you. You're a lovely girl, Leisal . . . and I'm only human.'

His cool, pleasant voice paused and Leisal looked up into those hypnotic, challenging eyes of his and smiled. He seemed completely relaxed now which was more than she could say for herself and she shook her head slowly. 'Damn you, James Lovell,' she murmured.

He reached out a hand and gently stroked

her cheek. 'Come on, let's go, it's getting late.'

Neither uttered a word until they were back at Hanaheen. James held his arm lightly around her waist as they entered the wood-panelled hall of the old house and when they reached the bottom of the stair he kissed her gently on her cheek, but he didn't attempt to caress her. The dusk was falling rapidly now and the thought of seeing James again later at dinner was very appealing.

Leisal turned to go up the stairs, and it was then she heard the sound of a door closing softly from the direction of the sitting-room. She turned quickly towards the sound, an unaccountable feeling of guilt rushing through her as she saw Aunt Harry walking stiffly along the hall towards them.

'I'm so glad you're home, James.' The woman's voice was choked with sobs. 'I didn't want to worry you, but I—'

James looked at his aunt with concern, recognizing a note of anguish in the thin voice, and when she swayed almost into a faint he moved quickly to hold her in his arms.

'What is it, Harry?' His tone was tender with concern as he held her tiny frame in the strong width of his arms. 'What's the matter?'

'Oh, James, I've been so silly. I'm afraid I've had one of my spells—I—I blacked out when you'd gone.'

'Blacked out?'

Harriet Lovell looked up at her nephew

with a wistful look in her blue eyes. 'I hope you aren't cross with me.'

'Cross with you? How could I be cross with you? Come on, I'll take you to your room and you can tell me all about it.' James steadied the old lady into his arms and guided her towards the stairs.

'Please—can I help?' Leisal moved forwards instinctively but immediately recoiled as though stung, when she saw the undeniable gleam of malice in the old lady's eyes. She froze in her tracks and remained where she was on the stair, but, just as suddenly, Aunt Harry's expression changed again swiftly as she looked at James, her tone thin and whining. 'Please, dear, I'll be fine when I've had a rest. Take me to my room.'

'Of course I will, darling.'

Leisal stood frozen in stunned disbelief as James helped his aunt up the stairs to her room. As he passed her, he turned his head for a brief moment and looked over the thin shoulder of his aunt, his eyes pleading with her. Suddenly Leisal felt very angry. How could he be so gullible that he couldn't see through the old lady's charade? She met his eyes levelly for that brief moment and then turned away, following them up the stairs and going quickly to her room, closing the bedroom door firmly.

CHAPTER FOUR

It was a little after 7.30 and Leisal sat at the dressing-table regarding herself critically in the mirror. It was almost time to go downstairs again, and she had to admit she was dreading spending any longer than she had to with Harriet Lovell. Her temper had cooled somewhat after spending a long time in the bath, and she wiled away the time trying to fathom out why the old lady had taken such an instant and ferocious dislike to her. After all, she was a paying guest, so why was Harriet being so rude?

Surely it couldn't be that she resented the interest James was showing in her? He was quite safe. She had no intention of stealing him away from his precious Hanaheen. All right, she accepted the attraction, but what was wrong with that? It didn't mean anything. Besides, she had no designs whatsoever on James Lovell—or any other man come to that.

Leisal glared at her reflection in the mirror and shook her tawny hair. Perhaps the old girl sensed it wouldn't be very hard for Leisal to fall in love with James Lovell. She bit her lip ruefully: not hard at all. And it was obvious that Harriet Lovell had plans for her nephew; plans that certainly did not include Leisal. But why all the theatricals? Why was she making such a big thing out of keeping them apart? Surely James could see through his aunt? Surely he could see the act she was putting on? And all that nonsense earlier about the fainting fit—the old lady was as strong as a horse.

Leisal's thoughts spiralled. Perhaps she was mistaken, and perhaps the rambling old house was doing things to her imagination.

She turned quickly, hearing a light step outside the door. Her heart leaped suddenly as she called for the person to come in, hoping for a moment it was James. But her heart sank like a stone when she recognized the visitor. It wasn't James. It was Harriet Lovell.

Aunt Harry looked around the room with the air of the hostess seeing to her guest's needs—even though they were unwelcome. And as Leisal warily regarded the old lady she had to admit that if the fainting attack *was* genuine then she seemed to have made a remarkably fast recovery for someone of her advanced years.

The old lady gave a slight sniff of distaste when she spotted the assortment of bottles and jars on the dressing-table. 'I hope you have everything you need.' Her remark held a note of sarcasm.

Leisal stood up quickly, turning to face the old lady. Their eyes met levelly. 'Yes thank you, Miss Lovell, I'm very comfortable, and I'm glad to see you're feeling better now.'

Harriet Lovell's indrawn breath was hardly audible and she glared at Leisal for a moment before saying, somewhat grudgingly, 'Much better, thank you. It's not at all like me to faint.'

Leisal made no comment as Harriet Lovell moved over to the window and looked out, taking deep breaths of air from the open window. Standing there, she reminded Leisal of a tiny porcelain doll, her blue china eyes staring out into the darkness and not a hair on her white head stirring in the breeze. Why had she come? Leisal knew that the visit wasn't for the sole purpose of expressing her concern for her guest's comfort.

Leisal waited for Harriet Lovell to make the next move. Presently, the old lady turned and said in a voice that reminded Leisal of cracked ice. 'So you followed your grandmother's footsteps and became an—*actress*?'

There was no mistaking the strongly disapproving emphasis on the word "actress" and it didn't go unnoticed by Leisal. She set her teeth, sitting down again and looking at the woman through the mirror of the dressing-table, answering coldly, 'You sound as though you don't approve, Miss Lovell.'

The old lady gave a slight shrug. 'My experience of your profession is very limited, but I've never been able to bring myself to trust an actress. Performers have always had a reputation for—well, shall we say living very freely ...? It must be quite comforting for an actress to marry someone of great wealth and standing. Many do, don't they? Someone like—well, like my nephew for example. To marry someone like James would make one feel very secure, wouldn't it? And helpful to their career?'

Leisal was outraged at the implication and she spun round on the old lady, her cheeks burning with indignation, but when she spoke her voice was cool and controlled. 'I would hope your nephew would have more sense than to choose a woman with such shallowness—that is, if he decided to marry at all.'

'Men can be such fools.'

'Not only men, Miss Lovell. We can all be foolish sometimes.'

'It's true though, isn't it, that men seem to have a weakness for actresses?'

'Do they? I don't know, I haven't thought about it.'

'Oh, yes. And my nephew is handsome—and well-off. And his head could be turned so easily by a pretty face, especially by one who could act the poor innocent girl needing to be looked after.'

Leisal turned her head back to the mirror and picked up her hair-brush, stroking briskly through her hair in an effort to control her rising temper. Harriet Lovell was quite ruthless, but also out-of-touch. James Lovell hadn't exactly struck her as a gullible man, one who would be easily taken in by a pretty face. For a moment she felt sorry for the old lady who had obviously been so dreadfully hurt in the past; so wronged that it jaundiced her outlook on everything, and could be very dangerous indeed. Especially for James. 'I shouldn't worry too much about your nephew, Miss Lovell,' she murmured. 'I'm sure he will choose the right girl when the time comes.'

'Enid is the right girl and he knows it. She's sensible, and of a *good* family. She would make him a good wife.'

'I'm sure she would,' Leisal murmured.

'Yes, well then, I'm sure you understand.'

'Understand?'

'Yes, I think we both understand, don't we, that it would be most improper of you to encourage my nephew with your actressy tricks.'

There was a long pause and when she spoke again Leisal's voice had taken on an unfamiliar coldness. 'With respect, Miss Lovell, I think you're over-stepping the line as my hostess, though I'll let it pass if only for my grandmother's sake. But for your peace of mind I don't need your nephew—or your nephew's money! I have more than enough of my own.' Then she added grimly, 'It's a pity you have such a bitter view of actresses, Miss Lovell.'

'I have reason to.'

'Your reasons are your own but I can assure you that your nephew is quite safe with me.'

'I speak as I find, and as far as I'm concerned, my nephew's future is my prime concern.'

Leisal replaced the hair-brush on its stand and turned to face the old lady calmly. 'Look, Miss Lovell . . .'

She said no more, however. Aunt Harry had turned her back and was walking swiftly towards the door, saying, as she went through, 'Dinner is in half an hour.'

When the door had closed behind her, Leisal stared at the wooden panels in incredulity, then she got up and went into the bathroom, picking up a tumbler from the shelf. She filled it with ice-cold water and rinsed her mouth several times, spitting the water back into the bowl in an effort to release the venom she was feeling for Harriet Lovell. She took three or four deep breaths and then went back to the dressing-table. Carefully she applied her make-up, adding less blusher than normal to her already hot cheeks, and then she combed her fingers through the tangled mass of curls.

'This is just too much!' she said aloud. 'Far, far too much!'

She was tempted to pick up the phone and book a seat on the first flight back to London. This was supposed to be a holiday, not a cat-fight with a bitter old woman. She didn't need this. But when she lifted the phone to dial the number of the airport, she paused, her finger hovering over the push-button. That would be too easy . . .

No! She'd be damned if she'd let the old woman drive her away! That was just what Harriet Lovell wanted! Instead, she walked over to the wardrobe and took out one of her favourite—and most revealing—dresses. Grape-dark lace, slit almost to the waist at each side, and hugging her slender hips like a sensual cobweb. One final check in the mirror and Leisal opened the door to go down for dinner. As she walked down the stairs she could almost hear the sound of the bell, and the words 'seconds out', as she entered the arena for the next round.

Through the half-open door of the sitting-room she could see James standing with his back to the door, glass in hand, talking animatedly to someone who was still out of Leisal's range of vision. She could hear the low murmur of voices and then Enid's clear laughter. When she went through the door Leisal felt again that strange, eerie feeling that time was suspended. She was aware of the strained silence as she entered the room and was conscious of their immediate attention as they turned to stare at her.

Enid was sitting by the open fireplace leaning elegantly against a cluster of cushions, glass in one hand and the other arm stretched casually across the back of the sofa. Harriet, motionless in a crimson leather chair, held Leisal with such a look of distaste that it bordered on discomfort. The glow of the lamp behind her cast a halo of golden light around her white head and, for a moment, James's aunt reminded Leisal of a withered old cherub.

Leisal felt strangely trapped. She felt a sense of relief when James moved swiftly to her side and slipped his arm around her shoulders, leading her forward to join the company.

He made no comment about her appearance but his look was enough.

'Leisal, at last. Can I get you a drink? Sherry? Scotch?'

'Sherry would be nice, please James. I'm sorry if I've kept you waiting.'

He handed her a sherry and introduced her to the two other occupants of the room, John and Catherine Drummond. They had driven over from Limerick earlier, she was told, and were staying in a small hotel in the village. James explained they were at Hanaheen for the express purpose of buying the new foal as an addition to their bloodstock.

The low murmur of conversation resumed and the atmosphere lost some of its tension as Leisal found herself button-holed by John Drummond on the problems of horse-breeding. She tried to listen attentively, but now and again she found her eyes wandering to the old lady in the crimson chair.

Two high spots of colour were burning in the old cheeks and, so far, she had not uttered a word. Leisal recognized the now-familiar chill of wariness wash over her. What was the old girl up to?

Her train of thought was interrupted, however, as she heard Enid's voice calling her name from her place at the fireplace. 'Leisal! Do you ride?'

She excused herself from John Drummond, who stood back with a polite little bow to resume his conversation with James. Throughout her conversation he had been standing patiently to one side and was watching her now with curious interest.

She turned her attention to the grey eyes of Enid. 'Yes, I do.'

'How would you like to take one of the horses out tomorrow?'

'I'd like that very much.'

'Then you can take Flora, she's gentle as a lamb. I'll get Mike to saddle her up for you in the morning.'

'Will you be coming with me?'

Was it Leisal's imagination again or did Enid's expression suddenly become guarded? She saw her throw a quick nervous glance towards the two men, a strangely disturbed expression on her face. But it was gone so quickly that Leisal wasn't sure if it had been there at all.

Enid turned her slate-grey eyes back to

Leisal. 'Sorry, no I can't. I'd love to but I'm afraid I have things to do.'

Leisal gave a slight indifferent shrug. 'Oh, well, perhaps, some other time.'

'Of course.' Enid threw another hurried glance towards James, then went on: 'And I'll get Mike to map out a decent ride for you—we'd hate you to get lost in one of our famed bogs, wouldn't we, James?'

Leisal saw the corners of his mouth lift into a slight sardonic smile. 'I'm glad to see that you're making sure Leisal makes the most of her stay at Hanaheen, Enid, but I'm afraid I'll have to throw a spanner in the works. I'd rather Leisal didn't go out alone, and besides, I had plans to take her to the island tomorrow.' He smiled his sudden warm smile and Leisal found herself smiling back.

'The island?' Enid's tone was full of questioning. 'But surely not, James. Why on earth would you want to take Leisal to the island?'

'Why not?'

'But—but there's nothing there, it's—it's deserted.'

'Exactly.' James threw Leisal a wink and laughed softly.

'Where is this island?' Leisal asked, looking first at James then at Enid. 'Is it far?'

John's wife, Catherine looked up with interest and broke in: 'Is that the island you can see from the coast road?'

James nodded. 'The Dancer's island?' Then to Leisal: 'Remember, I pointed it out to you when I brought you from the airport?'

She nodded, remembering the two giant statues that James seemed to admire so much. 'I remember.'

James grinned as he continued. 'I thought you said you wanted to get away from it all, and you can't get more away from it than on Dancer's Island. But if you'd rather ride . . .'

Before she could answer, Enid came elegantly across the room and casually placed her arm through James's. 'On second thoughts, it's a good idea, James, I'm sure Leisal would like to see the island.' She turned to Leisal. 'You can take Flora out some other time.'

James gave her a long look as he disentangled Enid's arm from his. 'That's settled then.'

Leisal laughed. 'You're spoiling me, all of you. You really are very kind, but I *am* quite capable, you know, of entertaining myself.'

'Of course you are,' grinned James. 'But I'd like to show you around, and I'm the most excellent company.'

'I've already discovered that.' Leisal's grin matched his.

'And don't worry, you'll be quite safe with me.'

'Will I?'

'Perhaps I'd better not answer that,' he said

levelly. 'You're going to have to find out for yourself.'

'I know him a great deal better than you, Leisal,' Enid broke in with a smile, 'and I can promise you, if he stays true to type, you're very safe. But remember, he's only on loan.'

He shot Enid a startled look. 'Why, Enid, you make me sound like something in a pawn shop. Anyway, I thought you were only interested in my mind.'

Enid's eyes narrowed. 'I'm interested in everything about my future husband, it's only natural. And I must be mad to let you loose tomorrow with someone as pretty as Leisal. It only goes to prove what a trusting soul I am.'

James turned to look at Leisal. The lamplight slanted across his face, sharpening the angle of his cheek-bones, and the look in his eyes unmasked a sign of bitterness that made Leisal catch her breath at the unexpectedness of it.

His voice, when he spoke again, was very quiet. 'Your trust is in safe hands, Enid.' Then suddenly his manner changed again and he laughed, a sudden gleam creeping into his eyes. 'What is it to be, Leisal? This island with me, or the peat bogs with Flora?'

They all laughed in great good humour. All except Harriet, that is. And as they moved out of the room to make their way into the dining-room Leisal was quick to spot the angry glare his aunt gave him as he slipped his arm around

Leisal's waist to lead her into dinner.

'It's not much of a choice, is it?' Leisal quipped. 'But I think, after all . . . that is, if you *really* don't mind, Enid, I'll go for the island.'

'Be my guest, but bring him back in one piece,' Enid invited airily, slipping her arm through John's.

'What did I tell you, Harry,' James laughed. 'Didn't I say these two would get on like a house on fire?'

'Yes, you did. Our guest is a very talented girl,' murmured Harriet and, innocent though the words were, they brought a sharp response from James.

'I don't think you know just how talented she is, Harry. Wait until you see her act.'

Harriet Lovell's eyes held Leisal spitefully. 'I believe I already have,' she said.

'Oh, but wait until you really see what I can do, Miss Lovell, I'm sure you'll be surprised,' Leisal assured her mockingly.

CHAPTER FIVE

Leisal awoke to a bright new morning. Hanaheen spread goldenly all around her, its silence relieved only by the faint breeze and the plaintive cry of the gulls. Waiting for James on the terrace, she looked out towards the moss-crowned crest of the cliffs.

In spite of everything she was feeling quite euphoric, breathing in the scent of earth and grass, her senses sharpened by the tang of the sea. Beyond the tall elms bordering the estate she could just make out the hazy blur of the Atlantic Ocean and Leisal knew how much she would miss the enchantment of this lovely place when her holiday came to its conclusion: a reluctant conclusion, in spite of Harriet Lovell's dislike of her.

'Leisal? Are you ready?'

Hearing James's call she looked back towards the house. He was standing by the door and her eyes were drawn to the expression on his face. It held a curious look. It was both impatient and wary at the same time. Behind him she saw the shadowy form of Harriet and it was clear they must have had words about his plans for the day with Leisal.

He came towards her, his white Aran sweater and denim slacks giving him an attractive nautical air. 'Come on,' he said, a distinct edge to his tone. 'Let's get to the boat and get out of here for a while.'

Taking the car, they zig-zagged down towards the tiny harbour, pulling up when they reached the wooden jetty. On the way, James's mood seemed to lighten and as they got out of the car he asked, 'Well, what do you think about her?'

At first Leisal thought he was referring to his aunt, but when she saw the proud gleam in

76

his eyes as he pointed to a stunning blue and white of a twin-masted boat, she realized he hadn't meant Harriet Lovell at all. Following his gaze her eyes swept along the hull, gasping at its sleekness and the thirty-eight foot or so of out-and-out luxury.

'Is this yours?' she asked, wide-eyed.

'Yes. Do you like her?'

'I'm impressed.'

James laughed. 'Impressed? Why? I thought all you movie people had boats.'

Leisal grinned ruefully, 'I haven't.' Her eyes swept the length of the boat. 'She's a beauty. What's her name?'

'*Lusty.*'

Leisal laughed out loud, her eyes dancing in amusement. 'You're joking?'

His good spirits restored, he chuckled, taking her hand and leading her aboard. 'Like owner—like boat. Here, take a look out there.'

He passed a pair of binoculars and Leisal peered into the far distance. Dancer's Island lay roughly six miles off the coast and through the powerful lens Leisal spotted the two stone statues which James had pointed out on that first day at Hanaheen. From this angle they looked even more human, their arms reaching out towards the sea as though beckoning unsuspecting sailors towards them—rather like she imagined the sirens to be when the Argonauts set out for the golden fleece. Handing back the binoculars she

77

acknowledged silently that she had never felt so peaceful, or so content, for a long, long time.

Once on their way, Leisal made coffee and they sat together at the table in the galley. She felt completely content, looking forward to spending a whole day with James and wondering what lay in store for them on his deserted island.

Her musings came to an abrupt halt, however, as James laid his hand on her arm and he said teasingly, 'A penny for them.'

She turned and looked at James Lovell. The handsome, intelligent face was smiling, and the dark eyes were almost black in the soft light from the porthole above his head.

Her eyes held his, her response vague. 'They're not worth a penny.'

'I think they are.' James looked at her for a long moment, his eyes thoughtful, but then he slowly broke into that broad smile which was becoming so familiar now: it lightened his whole expression. 'Tell me about it, what are you thinking? Is it about Tony?'

She snatched her hand away and looked at him darkly. 'That's not fair!'

Surprised by her swift anger James sat back quickly. He held up his hands in a gesture of surrender. 'Don't get so mad, I'm only curious.'

'Why did you have to bring Tony up? That's hitting below the belt. That's being devious, conniving and—'

'All right—all right,' James broke in hurriedly. 'I'm sorry. Let's forget it, shall we?'

'That's precisely what I'm trying to do.'

She broke off and reached for her almost-cold coffee, taking a long drink and draining the cup, then she sat back and examined James's grim face as he studied her from across the table. He gave a queer little twisted smile, then he said, quietly, 'I didn't mean to touch a nerve.'

'I know you didn't. It's just that Tony was the last thing on my mind just then, and suddenly—oh, I don't know—suddenly for a moment you brought it all back.'

James nodded. 'Yes, I can see that.' A moody darkness crept back into his expression and his eyes deepened. 'So, changing the subject as fast as I can, what will you do after—when your holiday is over?'

Leisal shrugged. 'Go back to work I suppose.'

'With Tony, and that crowd? Oops! Sorry again . . . That was thoughtless of me.'

The wide hazel eyes were expressionless as Leisal spread her long, delicate hands on the table and looked down at her fingernails. She shook her head slowly in a gesture of dismissal. 'There's talk of a sequel to *Sister of Judaea*—public demand and all that. Naturally, I'll be expected to play Sister Rosanna again.'

'And will you? Is that what you want?'

'Why not?' she murmured, not looking at him. 'It's a good part.' She shrugged elegantly. 'That's if we're able to make it at all. I hear the company's short of money again.' She threw him a rueful smile. 'Nothing new about that, of course, we're always over-budget. Anyway, if it does go ahead I believe it will be filmed in France: the climate's perfect there for movie-making.'

'In France? Where in France?'

'Provence, I believe—at least, that was suggested before I left.'

They fell into a short silence, and Leisal saw his hand make an abrupt movement of impatience. She lifted her head to look at him and saw the puzzlement in his eyes; but, at her glance, he turned away abruptly and made a pretence of examining the charts.

In a little over an hour the island came into view. First, the strangely flat, table-like tops of the craggy mountains; and then the giant formations of the rocks. It lay, mistily grey in the vast expanse of the ocean, and the shadows thrown by the sun drifted across the narrow valleys, the colours changing from muted browns and purples to bright reds and greens. Leisal stood with James at the wheel and watched as the granite dancers came into view, majestic and proud, overwhelming everything around them.

'Aren't they fantastic, Leisal?'

James's voice, quiet in her ear, sounded full

of wonder and respect as they stood together on the bridge of the *Lusty* under the shadow of the overhanging rocks.

She nodded. 'Yes, and a bit scary, too.'

He laughed. 'Come on, let me show you around.'

James moored the boat to the small landing-stage and the two of them set off up the steep angle of beach. The island was small, only three miles long and a little over half a mile wide; and, as they trudged its uncompromising terrain, James told Leisal how the island had once been bustling with a thriving community of monks. They were long gone now, of course. The plague had seen the last of them off over three hundred years ago. Now the only inhabitants were the wheeling, squawking gulls above their heads.

James caught hold of her hand automatically. 'I have a place here, we call it the lodge. Come on, I'll show you. It's just around this cliff.'

There was a light wind blowing in from the west and as Leisal followed James she had to admit that she was continually being surprised by this man. They walked side by side, laughing and talking, and James pointed out the various sea-birds as they swooped and wheeled above their heads. At last, they reached a stone-built dwelling nestling almost in the lap of one of the dancers. James opened a heavy wooden door and they stepped inside, their footsteps echoing emptily on the inlaid floor.

'So, this is where you run to when you want to get away from everything?' Leisal looked at him with her wide hazel eyes full of wonder. 'It's beautiful, James.'

He smiled. 'Come on, I'll show you the rest of it.'

The rest of the house lived up to its promise as James took her through the rooms one by one. At first there appeared to be only one floor, and the main room was the living room, furnished with heavy oak furniture and two huge divans set in an 'L' shape before an open fireplace, surprisingly warmly glowing now with logs and peat. There was a kitchen, and two beautiful bedrooms looking out over the wild craggy mountains at the rear.

But then, Leisal spotted a narrow staircase at the end of a passage, and which seemed to lead nowhere except on to the roof of the lodge. 'What's up there?' she asked.

James smiled. He was enjoying the admiration and open approval he could see in her eyes. 'That leads to my studio. That's where I go when I need to get away—far from the madding crowd.'

'May I see?'

'Of course you may.'

She followed him up the narrow stairway and into a room so light and airy that she felt she was on top of the world. The studio was built on top of the flat roof and was so spacious and comfortable that she felt she could live there in idyllic comfort forever. There was a fireplace and everywhere, in every available space, there were canvases and easels and palettes of oils.

'What a wonderful place,' she remarked, seating herself on the wide leather couch by the fire. 'I don't blame you for loving it so much.' She smiled up into his face. 'I could live here forever.'

'Perhaps!' He had been regarding her closely, his eyes watching her reactions and, as he spoke, his voice became almost a whisper. 'The lodge has been waiting for you . . . just as I have.' He hadn't meant to say that to her but she showed no reproof. Instead, she smiled and held out her hand. They sat down together on the couch and he took her hand gently, pulling her slowly into his arms and holding her close. It was entirely spontaneous, neither uttering a word for fear of disrupting the fragile enchantment that surrounded them.

They held each other for a long time, then he turned his face to hers, breathing her name. 'Leisal.'

She knew he was going to kiss her and she held her breath, waiting. Slowly, his mouth came down and suddenly he was kissing her with such a surge of love and tenderness that it fanned the flame already starting in her heart. 'Leisal . . . I'm . . .', he whispered again.

'Don't.' Her voice was the merest whisper. 'Please, James, don't say you're sorry ... I don't want you to be sorry.' She lifted her eyes to his and he could see the blazing passion that matched his own. 'I don't ... I've wanted you, too.'

'But, Leisal, there are things—'

She put her hand across his mouth. 'Ssh ...'

He kissed her again, bending tenderly over her and then lifting his head slightly, staring in wonder at her wide-eyed beautiful face. Slowly, not touching her with anything except his lips, he kissed her mouth again, so gently, so carefully: almost as though he was creating it. His touch was so full of wonder and love that she could hardly keep from screaming out loud, she wanted him so much. She pressed closer to him as he kissed her throat, her mouth, her hair. She was filled with an exquisite awareness, a realization that he was awakening feelings within her she had never felt before.

Then, just when she felt she could bear it no more, unexpectedly, she felt him pull away. 'Leisal.' His eyes held an anguished look as he faced her. 'I have no right ...'

'But ...'

'Do you honestly believe I could be happy with just an hour, a day, a week?' He shook his head slowly. 'I need a lifetime of you.'

'James ...'

He silenced her with another kiss then sat

back and took hold of her hand. His closeness was reassuring and the warmth of his body filled her with love. She snuggled against him on the couch and laid her head against the slow, even, rise and fall of his chest; and as they held each other she felt her heart take on a drowsy contentment.

She loved him! Whatever life had in store for either of them after this she knew she would love him for the rest of her life. She closed her eyes and listened to his heart beating in tune with her own; and as they sat together on the couch, she heard the steady beat of the rain as it started to fall on the glass panes above their heads.

'Tell me about the island, James,' Leisal asked softly. 'Tell me about the two dancers.'

'Not much to tell really.'

'I'd like to know just the same.'

He sat back contentedly. 'Well OK, if you insist.' She nodded and he smiled as he began to talk. 'No one's lived here for donkey's years—except the birds and the wild creatures, of course. It used to belong to the Cistercians but I don't think they knew quite what to do with it. It needed a hell of a lot spending on it to rebuild the abbey and, anyway, they have a huge monastery over at Caldey. Well, they decided to put it up for sale and, when I heard, I bought it like a shot.'

'Is Dancer's Island its real name? It doesn't sound very religious.'

He chuckled softly. 'No. It's really Hoy Island.'

'What about the dancers? Tell me about them.'

He kissed the top of her hair, his eyes narrowing into a smile. 'That's a very shady tale of love and jealousy.'

'Do tell me.'

He pulled her closer and ran his hands through her hair, settling himself more comfortably. 'Well, the old legend has it that hundreds of years ago—when this island was a sanctuary—a young lay brother fell hopelessly in love with a beautiful lady from the mainland.'

Leisal chortled. 'You should have started with "Once upon a time . . .".'

'This is a true story. Be serious please,' he chided jokingly, taking an apple from the fruit bowl by his side and biting deeply.

'Sorry,' smiled Leisal, taking a bite too. 'Please continue, I'll be quiet.'

'The lady was of noble birth and married to a man who was old enough to be her father. No one's quite sure how the young couple actually met, but when they did they fell headlong for each other. Women were forbidden on the island in those days, so in order to meet her lover, she would disguise herself as a boy and bribe one of her servants to ferry her over to the island when her husband had fallen asleep.'

'How romantic,' Leisal murmured, her imagination working overtime; and her heart with the two young lovers of long ago. 'Go on, James, what happened to them?'

He spread his hand in a wide gesture. 'It's said that this house was actually built on the very spot where they used to meet. He would play his lute, or lyre, or whatever they played in those days and she would dance for him. Then they would make love ... and make love ... and make love.'

'Yes, James, I've got the gist.'

He laughed again, twisting the ends of her hair through his fingers. 'Lucky devils.'

'Go on, James,' she cautioned. 'What happened to them?'

He grinned and went on. 'Unfortunately, the husband found out somehow that his wife did her disappearing act every night, and he didn't like it much. He was very curious, and I can't say I blame him. He was determined to find out what she got up to, so, one night, he followed her to the boat and saw her go over to the island. The next night he ordered the servant away and, disguising himself, he rowed his wife himself.'

James grinned at Leisal's rapt attention. He liked the way her head was resting on his shoulder and he liked the scent of the perfume in her hair. He watched her quietly for a moment until she murmured, 'Go on, James, don't stop.'

He continued quietly. 'Needless to say the inevitable happened. When her lover came to meet her, and he saw his wife go into her Salome routine, the old man became wild with jealous rage. He watched his wife make love to this young man in a way she never had with him and it sent him crazy. Suddenly he went berserk. He reached for his sword and plunged across the sand like a madman, then *swoosh!*' James raised his arm and brought it down swiftly into the arm of the chair. 'He plunged his sword into the heart of his wife's lover, killing him instantly.'

'Oh my goodness.'

James's voice rose to dramatize the scene. 'His hysterical wife threw herself prostrate on the ground in grief and, unable to face her adultery, the old man flung himself into the sea, never to be seen again.' His tone lowered theatrically. 'Just then, there was a great storm. A violent wind blew across the island, swirling like a hurricane and toppling the mountains. The wind lifted the tops of the mountains like matchsticks, pitching and tossing them until they crashed onto the beach below, hurtling down and destroying everything in their path. When, at last the storm abated and all was still, the two tragic lovers were entombed by the avalanche. As the centuries passed, the mountain-tops formed themselves into the shape of the two lovers, to dance forever on the sand—the Sand Dancers.'

'My, my, what a wonderful story.' Leisal sighed and stretched her arms. Then she giggled and completely shattered the atmosphere by adding practically, 'But it only proves my point.'

James got up, moving to the cabinet to open a bottle of wine. 'What point is that?'

'How dangerous love can be.'

He grinned, filling two glasses and carrying them over. 'You have no soul, Leisal Pavlova Leontina Adrianovitch.'

The night had grown cold when they set sail for the mainland. The night-wind stung Leisal's cheeks as she stood against the rails of the boat, straining her eyes to catch the last blurred contours of Dancer's Island before it disappeared in the distance. It had been a wonderful day. It was as though she had been caught up in a bright pink bubble and the real world was far away.

She felt herself shiver and hugged herself deeper into her denim jacket. The Dancers had disappeared into the dark mists of the evening and, all at once, Leisal found herself fighting off the feeling that her bubble would disappear too, once they returned to Hanaheen.

CHAPTER SIX

Mike was waiting anxiously for James as they drew up outside the door. He was pacing the driveway as though his life depended on it, 'You're needed at the stables, James, you'd better come straight away.' The man turned away and made a follow-me gesture with his hand.

'Is it the Princess, Mike?' James's manner was at once efficient and controlled.

Mike nodded sombrely. 'Yes, she's surprised all of us.'

Red Princess, the oldest brood mare, had gone into foal. She wasn't expected to give birth for another three weeks and Leisal knew that James was worried about her. 'Have you sent for Lionel?' he asked.

'Yes,' answered Mike. 'He's already here, and he's sent for the other chap, Sean Connolly, he's on his way from Drumcarrick— it's going to be a bit dodgy, James, the mare's not as young as she was.'

'Right, well, let's get going.' And giving Leisal a quick peck on her cheek, he said, 'Sorry, love, I'll have to leave you to your own devices tonight, this may take some time.'

'Can I help?' she asked.

'Thanks, but no. The mare doesn't know you, and it could only make her more distressed.' Then he added with a grin, 'But it's nice of you to offer just the same.'

Leisal shook her head helplessly, smiled, and said, 'Good luck, James.'

The two men left her standing in the doorway and, without a backward glance, sprinted across the field to the stables. Leisal stood watching them for a moment, then went indoors and made her way towards the stairs, looking forward to getting out of her clothes and taking a hot bath.

She was halfway up when she heard the soft brogue of Bridget's voice calling her from the door of the passage which led around the side of the conservatory. 'Is that you, Miss Adrian?'

Leisal turned to see the housekeeper standing just below her. 'Yes, Bridget?'

'Miss Lovell would like to see you, if you could spare her a moment?'

Leisal sighed. Here it comes, she thought, and looked down at the wrinkled face, 'Can't it wait until morning, Bridget?'

'She did say she'd like to see you now, miss.'

'Very well, where is she?' Leisal's tone was resigned.

'She's in her room, miss, she's been there all day.'

'All day? Why? Isn't she well?'

'No, miss.'

'What's the matter with her?'

The housekeeper shrugged her thin shoulders, her expression weary. 'I don't know, miss, but she's in one of her moods.'

The old lady turned away towards the door, and Leisal, knowing that she was about to face another confrontation with James's aunt, followed reluctantly.

Bridget led the way out of the hallway and down a corridor along the side of the house. The walls of the corridor were made entirely of glass and reminded Leisal of a goldfish bowl. Every few yards, patio doors opened up onto the magnificent gardens, and in the daylight, Leisal knew that the breathtaking views would stretch as far as the eye could see. At the end of the corridor they reached a white-painted door, and it was to this that Bridget led her. With a light tap Bridget opened it and motioned Leisal to go through.

The room was hot and humid, almost like a greenhouse, and filled with a varied assortment of exotic plants. Their perfume was heady, filling Leisal's nostrils with their scent and her eyes with their brilliant hues. In the centre of the room, Aunt Harry reclined on an old-fashioned *chaise-longue*, a book in her hand.

The old lady smiled weakly and gave a small flutter of her hand to Bridget as a sign of dismissal, then she turned to give Leisal a ghost of a smile, saying in a small complaining voice, 'Leisal, dear girl, how nice of you to spare the time to see me.'

When Bridget had gone, she beckoned

Leisal to come nearer, and as Leisal stepped warily forward she tried hard not to show her dismay at the old lady's condition. She was pale, and the thin hand was holding a compress against her forehead.

'I'm sorry you're not feeling well, Miss Lovell.'

The old lady made no response as she put the compress down on to the table by her side and helped herself to a grape from a silver dish. Then she made a gesture with her fragile hand, the enormous sapphire ring on her third finger gleaming in its old-fashioned setting and reflecting the light from the lamp. 'Come, Leisal, sit here by me.'

She patted vaguely to a space by her feet and Leisal moved slowly forward and sat down. The two women eyed each other, neither giving an inch. A faint trace of malice hovered on Harriet's lips, and the old eyes flashed as she met Leisal's level gaze. Leisal felt two bright spots of colour come to her cheeks as she recognized the well-controlled rage which burned inside the woman's breast.

'Is James with the mare?', the thin voice asked at last.

Leisal nodded, 'Yes, and Mike; and the vet's with her, too, so she's in good hands.'

There was a long pause while Harriet Lovell laid back her head on the pillows and closed her eyes, then after some moments a soft colour came to the old cheeks as she asked

93

with feigned interest, 'Did you enjoy Dancer's Island today?'

'Very much.'

Harriet Lovell reached for another grape, giving Leisal a cool glance. 'I was surprised when I heard James had taken you there, he usually likes to go off alone.'

'He wanted me to see the Dancers.'

There was a short pause, then Harriet Lovell frowned and she shook her head impatiently. 'I have to be honest, I don't like it. I don't like it at all.'

'Why? It's been a perfect day.'

'He has no right to spend so much time alone with you—people will talk.'

Leisal smiled. 'There's nothing for them to talk about.'

'You don't understand. Perhaps it's nothing for people like you to go off alone for hours on end, but we Lovells are a proud and distinguished family.' Her tone seemed to bite off each word. 'We have a position to maintain, and we take great pride in maintaining it.'

'How very nice,' said Leisal drily.

'Are you being impertinent?' Harriet's eyes burned angrily.

'I hadn't intended to be, but I'm sure you didn't ask to see me so late in the evening just to tell me that.'

The cold blue eyes held Leisal's. 'No, I didn't. What I wanted to see you about does concern my nephew though.'

'Yes?'

'I don't like the way he's spending all his time with you.'

Leisal gazed steadily back into those cold blue eyes, 'I rather think that's up to James, don't you?'

'No, I don't. James is meant to marry Enid and I don't want you to do anything to spoil their future.'

Leisal looked at the thin, intelligent face, chalk-white now in the light of the lamp. 'It isn't my intention to spoil James's future.'

'But that's exactly what you *are* doing.'

'Miss Lovell,' began Leisal patiently, 'I really think that James can decide for himself. Whatever plans he has for his future are his own. I'm certain he will make all the right decisions when the time comes.' She stood up, looking down at the old lady lying so apparently helpless on the old-fashioned *chaise-longue*. 'And I didn't come here to argue with you again. I'd rather hoped we could be friends, but I can see now that we can never be. If that's all you wanted to discuss then I suggest you talk it over with James. Goodnight, Miss Lovell, I hope you feel better in the morning.'

'How can I feel better when I have so much to worry about?'

'You have nothing to worry about—except perhaps your own imagination.'

'You encourage him.'

Leisal sighed deeply. 'Please, Miss Lovell, don't push me into saying something I shall regret later.'

The old lady's eyes were red with rage. 'I hate to think what will happen now. You're turning his head with your scheming ways.'

'Miss Lovell, I've already told you—I haven't come here to quarrel with you!' Leisal walked towards the door, her outrage almost impossible to contain. She didn't know how much longer she would be able to remain polite to this insufferable old woman, who was still speaking from across the room.

'I hope you're proud of this day's work: you've upset me very badly.' And then, her voice filled with venom, she added, 'If you stay here and entice my nephew into marriage I shall personally see to it that he loses everything! You are no good for him! You will only break his heart! Enid is the one for him!' Then with eyes as cold as ice she spat, 'Go back to the rest of your kind in London where you belong—you're not wanted here!' Harriet Lovell clasped a hand to her bosom, her breath coming out in short, painful gasps. 'You don't love him, you only want his money, his name. I warn you, I shall do everything in my power to see that you don't ruin his life.'

Leisal didn't wait to hear any more. She opened the door and walked through quickly, closing it firmly behind her. Alone in her

96

room, she sat on the edge of her bed, her thoughts spinning around in a whirl. A hot surge of anger was sweeping through her like a raging tide as she remembered the words the old lady had spat: 'Go back to London where you belong—you're not wanted here!'

Why on earth did Harriet Lovell despise her so much? What was it about her that sparked off so much hatred? Leisal shook her head in bewilderment and rubbed her temples with her fingertips. She got up and moved to the dressing-table, narrowing her eyes as she examined herself in the mirror. Despite the fatigue that was pulling at her, her thoughts turned to James, and of the deep love for him that had blossomed in the brief few days she had known him.

Leisal tried to make some sense of it. She hadn't made love to a man in over a year. Was that why she was so attracted to James? Was it merely physical? And was she misinterpreting these overwhelming feelings as love? She didn't think so. Physical attraction was easily recognizable, and pleasant as it was, this warmth she felt for James went much deeper than that; deeper than anything she had ever known, or imagined she had known before in her life. Would she ruin his life? Would she one day wish to return to her career and break the continuity of this old and proud family? Is that what Harriet Lovell was afraid of?

And if it was something else entirely, what

97

on earth could it be? Obviously, the old lady had her reasons. Was it some sort of unhealthy possessiveness? Jealousy, even: that the old lady was afraid he would leave her alone? Maybe the fact that James's attention towards her was stirring up some old hatred that Leisal would never understand.

She shook her head again. Whatever it was would have to wait. It was too late in the day to worry about it now, not that she could do much about it anyway. She stood up slowly and undressed. Her bubble had certainly burst but perhaps, she told herself, it would all look different in the morning. A little while later, when she was bathed and in bed she turned out the light. She reached her arm along the pillow, wishing . . .

In spite of Harriet Lovell she wished with all her heart that her arm held the warm, comforting body of James Lovell.

Sleep overtook her at last, and when it came it was the kind of sleep that only comes when the mental and physical efforts of the day bring utter exhaustion. It was a restless, troubled sleep, haunted by dreams of a young monk and a beautiful lady, dancing on the sand below an old abbey. And although she couldn't see the face, she knew that the dark, sinister figure watching the lovers as they danced in the shadow of two giant rocks, had the face of Harriet Lovell.

Stirring, Leisal awoke to a room flooded

with sunshine, and she could hear the noisy clamour of birds in the trees outside her window. A little after eight o'clock she went down for breakfast, to find a bulky package awaiting her on the table in the hall. It was the script for the sequel to *Sister of Judaea*, and as she opened the reinforced envelope she found a hurriedly scrawled message from Tony. *Say you'll do it, sweetie, we'll get the money somehow. Don't let me down, PLEASE!!!* It was as though fate had stepped in and made her decision for her.

'Don't tell me I've forgotten your birthday.'

She glanced up quickly to find James standing barely three yards from her in the doorway. She'd been so engrossed in Tony's letter and the script that she hadn't heard him come in.

With a start she answered quickly, 'No, James, it's not my birthday, it's my new script, that's all.'

He stepped forward and closed the door behind him. She sensed something in his manner which was very hard to read, and there was a redness around his eyes which suggested he'd slept very little, too.

He didn't respond for a few moments and when he did his voice was tense. 'Are you going to do it?'

'I think so, it's a good part.' Leisal deliberately kept her tone light. Then, changing the subject quickly, she asked, 'How's the mare?'

'She's fine.'

'And how's your aunt this morning?'

He took her arm and led her into the dining-room. For an instant Leisal saw the bright flash come into his eyes, then it was gone, and his voice when he spoke was calm and even, 'She's going to be all right. Doctor O'Brian has just left, he's given her another sedative.'

Leisal reached out a tentative hand and touched his arm, asking solemnly, 'James, what exactly is the matter with your aunt?'

His face tautened. 'I'm not really sure. O'Brian seems to think she's getting herself over-excited about something, although I can't imagine what. But I sometimes forget just how delicate she can be.'

'Delicate' was the last word Leisal would have chosen to describe the formidable old lady who happened to be his aunt, but she made no comment. Instead, they strolled together into the dining-room, James seating himself with a boiled egg, and she pouring some coffee into two cups, listening attentively as he continued. 'Harry took over the reins of Hanaheen when my mother died. She looked after me, and the house, and everything connected with the estate. She's given her whole life to Hanaheen—and to me, I owe her a lot.' He grinned slightly, taking a gulp of his coffee. 'Anyway, enough of my life's history, what shall we do today? Do you feel like riding?'

She smiled, trying to act naturally. 'Not today, James, I have things to do.'

He gave a hard little laugh. 'Had enough of me already?'

'No, it's not that, James. I—I think it's time I got back to work.'

'Nonsense!'

'I mean it, James.'

'Well, of course, if that's what you want.' His voice had gone flat and dead. The air around them hung as heavy as lead until James, taking hold of her hand, said softly, 'Stay here, Leisal. Stay here and marry me.'

Leisal's breath caught in her throat. It was the moment of truth!

She wanted to scream out loud that Yes! Yes! she would marry him right now!

But then Harriet Lovell's thin face broke into her thoughts and instead, reason taking over, she stammered, 'Please—James, you're going much too fast.'

He smiled, holding her hand gently and bringing it to his lips. 'Not fast enough.'

'I'm trying to be serious.'

'So am I.'

'I mean it. I've decided to go back to work tomorrow.'

She sensed, rather than felt, his involuntary movement. His mouth tightened and he let go of her hand abruptly, his voice once again took on that hardness and around his mouth came faint, bitter lines. 'I see.'

'I don't think you do. Please understand, James, it's all for the best.'

He shot her a look that spoke volumes. 'The best for whom?'

'For both of us.' Her voice trailed away weakly.

She felt her heart twist uncomfortably under his gaze, and the brief shadow of strain made his eyes look enormous. 'Something's wrong, isn't it?'

'Of course not.'

'Leisal—can't you put it off?'

'No.'

His expression became stony. 'Are you sure it's work you're going back to, or is it Tony?'

Leisal's eyes lifted to his, wide and darkened with a flash of anger. 'That's an insult, James. Is that what you think?'

'What else am I to think?' He was looking deep into her face, the light from the window catching a slant of puzzlement in his dark eyes. Then he reflected soberly, 'I'm sorry, Leisal, the last thing in the world I want is to insult you, it's just that I can't stand the thought of you with someone else.'

Leisal shrugged, trying to climb through the mountain of disappointment that was settling upon her. When she left this place she would have to live with the fact that he would probably marry Enid, and she couldn't stand the thought of that, either. She kept her voice deliberately light, and said, jokingly, 'I do have to earn a living.'

'Oh, come on, love, I'm not buying that, there's something else, isn't there?'

She twisted away, moving across to the window. How could she explain his aunt's hostility without appearing to be cruel. Besides, it was happening all too fast, perhaps he only believed himself in love with her and would be more suited to Enid after all. They both needed time.

She stood silently for a moment, looking out, then she turned slowly and met his eyes. 'I feel I want to go back to work, isn't that enough reason?'

James stiffened, his eyes narrowing as they held her in their gaze, then he spoke without emphasis, but Leisal felt as though the words were being hammered on cold steel. 'No, Leisal, it isn't. Why this sudden desire to get back to work? I have plans for us.'

Leisal gave a small, desperate laugh and turned away from the window and back towards the table again. 'Hasn't it occurred to you that I might love my job, and miss it?'

He let the question hang, and in the silence that followed, without looking at him, Leisal opened her bag and took out a photograph of herself. She signed it quickly and handed it to James. 'It's for Joe. Will you give it to him for me?'

James glanced at her picture, running his fingers along the glossy cheek, then he looked at Leisal and smiled. 'All right,' he said at last, with a return to his old careless manner. 'If there's nothing I can do to make you change your mind.'

Leisal smiled back and shook her head in reply. 'Nothing at all,' she murmured quietly.

He reached out a hand and touched hers gently. 'I had a feeling that we shared something, that we were on the way to finding something very special.'

She closed her hand over his in an effort to allay the tormenting emotions his touch was kindling. 'I believe it's called lust,' she grinned.

'Then I lust you very much, Leisal.'

She smiled sadly, 'You'll soon get over it, James.'

He bent towards her kissing her face softly. Leisal closed her eyes, aware of the lurch of her stomach as her body responded to his touch. His hands moved in a pleasurable quest along her slim back, gliding tantalizingly over her thighs, tormenting her, and his fingers touched just enough of her to make her burn for more.

She pulled away quickly. 'Please, James don't.'

'Don't go, Leisal, stay with me.' He gazed broodingly into her eyes, his voice becoming low and husky with emotion. 'I don't know what you're doing to me, Lord knows I don't.'

His fingers gently read her face, not missing a detail, tracing the contours of her silky skin. 'I used to have my life under control. I always knew what I wanted, and where I was going, but now . . .'

'Please, James, leave me now and let me pack.'

He took her in his arms, his voice barely audible above her beating heart. 'I could ask you to stay with me tonight at least, but I won't. I won't ask you now. When you come to me I want all of you, your body, your mind, and, most of all, your heart. But if your work comes before all of that, then so be it.'

'It does,' she lied.

He stiffened, letting his hand drop hopelessly to his side and his eyes hurt and angry. 'I'd better see to the Princess before I do something I'll regret—we'll talk about this later.'

James moved away towards the door, almost colliding with Enid as she came through. 'Hello, James, any coffee going?' Enid looked quickly at the two of them, sensing she'd come into the room at the wrong moment. 'Sorry, you two, have I interrupted something?'

'No, I was just leaving.' James shot Leisal a long look, and then he turned and strode briskly out of the room.

Leisal let out a sigh and sat back in the chair as Enid helped herself to coffee. 'What was all that about, or is it none of my business?' she asked, joining Leisal and swinging her long legs under the table.

Leisal shrugged slightly, 'It was—it's nothing.'

'Oh, come on, Leisal, you can't fool me,' Enid chided cheerfully. 'Don't tell me you're having trouble with dear old Aunt Harry.'

Leisal stared in surprise. 'What made you say that? Why on earth should I?'

Enid laughed. 'Don't be afraid to admit it, she's been on your back about James, hasn't she?'

Something in Enid's tone made Leisal glance sharply at her. 'I thought you liked her.'

'Of course I like her, I've known her all my life, and I respect her. But I know what she can be like, I've seen her in action,' admitted Enid frankly.

'Well, I must admit, I distinctly get the impression that she isn't exactly over the moon about my being here.'

'Leisal, for heaven's sake, don't let her suspect that or your life won't be worth living—she can be quite a bully. And for that advice I'm not going to apologize. Just be on your guard, that's all, she'll try to break up any attachment you may have with James.'

Leisal sat very still for long moments, watching the girl across from her at the table, then she asked quietly, 'Is that the reason you and James are not married yet?'

Enid's face became a taut mask, and she moistened her lips with the tip of her tongue before she answered. 'The one and only reason I haven't married James yet, is that James hasn't actually asked me.'

Leisal's heart sank a little. 'Then you *are* in love with him.' It was a statement of fact, not a question.

Enid turned puzzled eyes to Leisal. 'In love? What's love got to do with it?'

It was Leisal's turn to look puzzled. 'But what other reason would you have?'

Enid shrugged. 'Plenty of them. The Lovells have wealth, power, security, social prestige, luxury, you name it and they've got it, and there's the added privilege of spitting in Aunt Harry's eyes.' That thought caused Enid to grin suddenly, then she went on. 'Seriously, there's a lot to be said for marrying James, and especially for someone like yourself ... acting can be a dodgy business, can't it?'

'Life itself can be a dodgy business, Enid, and I've already made up my mind to stay with acting.' Then Leisal added softly, 'But, if I ever did marry, it wouldn't matter if he was as poor as a church mouse, just as long as we loved each other.'

Enid grinned a small crooked smile. 'How sweet. And how old-fashioned. But I'll admit, Leisal, you've put me in my place.' Enid's tone was without rancour as she went on. 'I always meant to marry him, I'll be honest about that.

I always felt I would but somehow he just kept slipping away from me. Now', she gave Leisal an odd look, 'I may as well forget him. He's slipped away for good, so there's no point in my sulking. Anyway, I wish you well, Leisal, and there are plenty more fish in the sea for me.'

'Thank you, Enid, and I wish it had been different for you.'

Enid chuckled. 'It doesn't matter. I'll admit, when you first came here I felt a little jealous. But if it hadn't been you, it would have been someone else. I don't honestly believe that James ever looked on me as his future wife, we're too much like brother and sister.'

Leisal eyed her for a moment, then she nodded soberly. 'Well, I'll be gone in the morning, then perhaps you can all get back to normal.'

'Gone? But your holiday's only half way through. Where are you going?'

'Back to work.'

Later, upstairs in her room, Leisal took out some writing paper and wrote a long letter to her grandmother. Talking to Boushka always helped. And when the letter was finished she propped the envelope against her bag on the table and reached for her suitcase. The sooner she went back to work, the sooner she would be able to get James Lovell, Hanaheen, Aunt Harry, and all the rest of it out of her mind.

CHAPTER SEVEN

Southern France was hot. Leisal stretched her suntanned legs along the striped canvas of the footstool, settling back in the bamboo chair. She opened her book but didn't read. Instead, she looked about her. The shade from the balcony's awning gave her a little respite from the fierce heat and, in the tinderdry trees around her, she could hear the incessant monotonous rasping of the cicadas.

The air was filled with the heady perfume of the jasmine covering the wrought-iron rails of the terraced garden. A few people were taking some refreshment at the umbrella-bedecked tables beneath her balcony, but even they seemed motionless in the torpid heat of the late afternoon. Nothing stirred. Not even a breeze disturbed the still water of the River Rhone below. She gazed down at the winding ribbon of golden light, the gleaming water reflecting the sun-bleached stone of the arches that spanned its banks, and she found her thoughts straying inevitably to James.

She had said goodbye to Hanaheen in the cold grey light of an Irish dawn. And yet even now, after almost three months, the image of his face swam before her eyes in her unguarded moments. Her mind went back to that last morning before she left for France.

To Aunt Harry's triumphant wave of farewell; a wave which still rankled bitterly inside her heart. And to the memory of James's tense cheek against hers at Shannon as he kissed her goodbye, reminding her savagely that perhaps she was a fool to leave him.

'How far is Avignon?,' he had questioned her softly, holding her eyes with his challenge.

'Not far. Two, perhaps three hours by air at the most.'

She had felt his body beside her, holding her and pulling her close. 'Two hours—or two thousand hours—they won't be enough to separate us. You know that, too, don't you Leisal? But, if you must, then go to France and act your part in the charade, I can't stop you, and I'm not going to try. It's your life, and when you come to me I want you to be absolutely sure that it's what you want.'

She smiled a little. Was it really eleven weeks ago?

At first, when she arrived at the film's location, she'd been too busy to think about her sadness. She'd quickly become absorbed into the pace and excitement of making a television series, half of her submerging into the tragic character of the nun of Tony Sheraton's imagination, and the other half forcing Hanaheen, and all it meant to her, out of her mind. But now, with most of her schedule complete, she had more time, and all her thoughts had become centred on James

Lovell, and how she was missing him.

There were a couple of re-takes to do and the final scene to shoot, and *Sister of Judaea— The Conclusion* would reach its inevitable wind-up.

She frowned, and offered up a little prayer that trouble wouldn't rear its head before the final scenes were shot. It usually did at this stage and, in spite of the incredibly good ratings of the first series, money was running out fast. Tony was at this very moment in London chasing for more, and Leisal hadn't the slightest doubt that he would come up with the necessary backing. Even if it meant changing some of the script to suit someone's overblown ideas of production, he'd find it somehow.

His greatest strength lay in his flexibility in manipulating the stranglehold of the budget, without forfeiting that special magic of his direction. His phone call, when he had rung her on the set that morning, had sounded promising. 'Leisal, have you ever heard of Talbotson International?'

'Yes, I think so. Aren't they into copper or something?'

'They're into almost everything.'

'What about them?'

'I think I've persuaded them to lend us a few quid.'

'I knew you'd do it, I knew you'd get it from somewhere.'

'It was no problem. As a matter of fact, they approached me. Said they wanted to move into television and heard we needed more finance.'

'Wonderful!'

'That's why I'm ringing you: they're sending someone to Avignon today to look around while I do some negotiating here, will you look after him for me?'

Leisal smiled to herself. She knew as far as Tony was concerned she was one of his best assets. And if Talbotson International could be sweetened with the promise of being shown around by the star of the show—none other than Leisal Adrian herself—then he would use her for that purpose.

'It's the least I can do, Tony. What time is he arriving? And at which hotel will he be staying?'

'He'll be there some time this afternoon. He's catching the 1.30 plane from Gatwick. And the hotel is the George Rene, OK?'

'Right. I'll telephone the hotel this evening and arrange to meet him tomorrow on the set. It'll give the man a chance to settle in.'

'No, Leisal.' Tony's voice was crisp and confident. 'It's all arranged. I've already half-promised that you'll see him tonight—around eight o'clock'—there was the briefest pause— 'and have dinner with him.'

Leisal frowned her annoyance. One of the most irritating things about Tony was that he took her acceptance so easily for granted.

Knowing that, she chafed, 'I do wish you wouldn't arrange things like that, Tony. You should have given me more warning. I honestly don't feel like entertaining a complete stranger tonight.'

'Please—it's important.'

She sighed, exasperation revealing itself in her tone. 'Do I have a choice?'

'Not really . . . not if we want to finish the series on time.' She sensed the grin on his face at the other end of the phone, then he went on: 'He seems a nice guy, and it's only dinner I'm asking you to have with him. I chose the short straw, remember, persuading him to part with the money. Will you do it?'

'Yes, I'll do it,' she replied resignedly. 'What's his name?'

'Talbotson.'

'The boss himself?'

Tony laughed. 'No other. Thanks, Leisal, I'll see you in a couple of days.' And then he'd rung off.

Hazily now she turned her head away from the startling light of the sun and went inside, cooling her damp forehead with some iced water from the carafe by the bed. The silence and coolness of the room subdued her irritation somewhat and, lying down on the four-poster, the image of James glowed and faded in her mind's eye.

She wondered what he was doing, and if he was thinking of her, too. She sat up on her elbow and reached into the drawer by her side to take out a small bundle of letters, opening them and reading them for the hundredth time.

James's first letter had come quite soon after her arrival at Avignon, and the sight of the Hanaheen postmark was enough to send her scurrying to her dressing-room to read it in privacy. It was a pleasant, friendly, and completely casual letter, and when she'd read it she'd put it down with a feeling of deflation. It asked after her career, her health and other things, but there was nothing to bring a tingle to her heart—not even between the lines.

She had taken out her writing-paper and after four attempts had finally got the right tone in her reply. It was as casual and friendly as his had been, and when she had finished she had read it through several times to make sure there was nothing he could find between the lines either. She had put it to one side and posted it three days later.

Not once had he telephoned. Other letters had arrived during the first three weeks, just as friendly as the first, beginning with 'Dear Leisal' and ending, 'James', or, 'sincerely, James.' Then the letters's content became shorter and shorter and more infrequent, until now they seemed to have petered out altogether. She hadn't heard a thing from him in three weeks, and that, it seemed, was that! For all his talk of love, it seemed that the magic of Ballyhoe and the sensuous writhing of the Dancers had blurred into a pleasant memory.

Oh, well, it had been nice while it lasted. She put the letters back in the drawer, forcing herself to put him out of her mind and concentrate entirely on her career. She smiled a little ruefully to herself. Her career! It all depended on Tony now, and if he could come up with enough money from Talbotson International to make sure she had a career.

Today had been tough, and she was enjoying the break after the day's shooting. Tonight might be even tougher: having dinner with a stranger, and one she didn't particularly want to meet. Leisal turned her head towards the window, knowing that time was passing quickly, and she'd better make a move if she was to keep her appointment at the Hotel George Rene. She felt a small shock of surprise when she saw that the sky was now inky black, and that darkness had fallen with the sudden swiftness of a southern night; a swiftness that never failed to startle her. She glanced at her watch, it was almost seven o'clock. She got up and walked over to the balcony to close the white wooden shutters, then she went into the bathroom to get ready for dinner.

A little after eight o'clock, Leisal stepped out of a taxi and walked through the ornate oak-polished doors of the Hotel George Rene and to the reception desk. Clutching a small black evening-bag in her left hand, she stepped forward confidently, her tall well-formed shape gracefully enhanced by the clinging fire-silk dress. The look of unconcealed approval in the eyes of the young man behind the desk corresponded with the glances of the people sitting or standing around in the hotel foyer.

'I have an appointment with Mr Talbotson,' she informed him quietly.

The desk clerk smiled, 'Mademoiselle Adrian?'

'Yes.'

'Will you follow me please, Mademoiselle?'

He led her past the restaurant which was now quickly filling up for dinner, and Leisal was aware of the glances of the diners as she passed by: glances that were part recognition, part appreciation of her striking looks, and part curiosity. The reception clock pointed at a few minutes past 8.15, and as Leisal followed the silent form of the man she wished she was back in her room at her hotel. It wasn't the fact that she was having dinner with a stranger, she was quite used to that, but she wished she hadn't given in to going at all. It would have been a simple matter to have choked Tony off and met the man tomorrow. But perhaps that would have given offence and he was trying his best to raise money.

The man ushered her into one of the lifts and pushed the button for the third floor.

They passed no word to each other as the lift carried them silently upwards, and when they got out he led her along a thickly carpeted corridor until at last he reached his destination.

He tapped softly on the door of number 351 and, without waiting for a reply, he opened it, standing to one side for Leisal to go through.

She smiled her thanks at the man and went in only to stop short at the scene which awaited her. The room was spacious, and elegantly furnished, but in spite of the luxurious setting, it was intimate. A table had been laid for two in a recess at one of the long old-fashioned windows; heavy folds of rich green velvet, looped together by huge gold tassels, hung at the windows, closing out the night. Champagne waited in an ice-bucket and candles glowed from their burnished holders in the centre of the table.

Leisal stood gazing round in amazement. This wasn't what she had in mind when she'd agreed to dine with Mr Talbotson. This had been deliberately planned for a romantic tête-à-tête. Suddenly she felt an unreasoning surge of anger towards Tony that he should include seduction as part of the deal. She turned back towards the door but stopped abruptly as a man's disembodied, yet strangely familiar voice came from the balcony. 'Thank you, Gervase.'

The man, Gervase, gave another small bow

and left, closing the door discreetly behind him.

Leisal turned her face towards the voice and, after a moment, a tall casually clad figure, wine-glass in hand, stepped easily into the room from the balcony.

'Hello, Leisal,' said James Lovell. 'How nice to see you again.'

Leisal could only gasp, totally at a loss for words. The sight of him jolted through her like an electric shock and she stood there frozen. Then initial shock gave way to conjecture and with a supreme effort of control she made her voice toneless and asked, 'James, what on earth are you doing here?'

He smiled faintly at her questioning gaze. 'A reward for my persistence. Are you so surprised?'

She gulped, gathering herself. '*Surprised?* Honestly, James, you're the master of understatement.'

'I hope I haven't overdone it, you look as if you've seen a ghost.'

He put his glass down on a small bar and in a few strides he was standing by her side, taking her hands in his, and kissing her first on one cheek and then on the other.

Leisal laughed a little nervously. 'It *is* a bit like seeing a ghost,' she acknowledged. 'But I suppose I should be used to your surprises by now.' She took a small step back and faced him squarely. 'James, what are you doing here?'

Grinning lazily he ushered her towards the dining table. 'What's the matter? Aren't you pleased?'

'Well, of course I am. Very pleased. But, James—how in the world . . . ?'

'No "hows".'

'But—'

'No "buts" either. Our dinner will get cold.'

'Dinner? But—I can't stay here—I can't have dinner with you.'

'Oh, yes you can.' He gave a sweep of his hand, indicating the beautifully set table between them. 'As you can see, it's all prepared.'

'But, really—honestly, I can't.'

'Why not?'

She shook her head. 'Because I happen to be having dinner with a man called Talbotson. I thought—'

'Don't argue with me, Leisal . . . sit down, please.' James held her chair while she sat down and then poured some wine into her glass, his attractive teasing eyes catching the light of the candles. 'Talbotson? A friend of yours?'

'No—I don't know. It's someone Tony's met, and it's important that I have dinner with him. James—'

She made a move to stand up but James laid a restraining arm on her shoulder until she sat down again. 'Relax, Leisal, I'm sure this chap

119

Talbotson will understand.'

She looked quickly into his face. There was something in his tone which made her eyes wide with questions. She had a feeling he was playing with her. That he knew more than he appeared to. She asked in a curious tone, 'You know something about it, don't you?'

'It's really quite simple,' James chuckled.

'I don't follow you.'

He reached across the table, taking hold of her hands and saying quietly, 'That's precisely my problem. That's exactly what I want you to do. I want you to follow me.'

She held his gaze. 'James ... there's something going on, isn't there? Something I don't know.' She was totally perplexed but even through her bewilderment she was happy in the silent joy of seeing him again. What was he doing here? Leisal's curiosity brought her back to reality. 'Tell me, James,' she murmured.

'All right, I'll tell you everything.' He grinned mysteriously, as though hugging a secret deep inside. 'You do realize you're in the company of a genius, don't you?'

'I believe you've mentioned it a couple of times,' she smiled in return. 'Now, are you going to tell me, or not?'

'All right,' he said again. 'I'll tell you.' He took a long breath and grinned impishly, 'During the last couple of years your TV company has suffered a few losses, hasn't it?'

Leisal nodded. 'I'm afraid so,' she admitted dispiritedly. 'We've all put quite a lot of our own money into it, but it's been like a drop in the ocean.'

'I know. Now you need new capital, and the bankers are being cautious about lending more money, especially to companies like yours whose balance-sheets are unimpressive to say the least.'

'You seem to know a lot about it.'

Expressionless now, he said smoothly, 'I made it my business to.'

Leisal gave a low throaty laugh, 'Is there anything you don't know about me?'

'Not much.'

His fingers stroked across her hands, caressing, almost as though he was already loving her. Leisal made an instinctive movement to respond, then checked as her mind began to function again. 'And Mr Talbotson? Do you know anything about him?'

James smiled. 'In a way.'

'Go on, James.'

'I was worried.'

'About me?' she asked, trying to ignore the way his touch was awakening feelings again. 'Or about Mr Talbotson?'

The candle-light spilled across her breasts and shoulders, and onto him, and the look in his eyes told her that the time that had passed between them over these past few weeks had done nothing to dampen the need they both felt for each other.

'Yes, to both counts,' he replied in his quiet way.

'There's no need to worry about me, James,' she said, 'but what about Mr Talbotson? He'll be waiting for me somewhere, and—'

'No, he won't.'

She looked into his face with surprise. 'How do you know?'

'I know, because I'm Mr Talbotson.'

Leisal stared at him, not knowing what to say. Her eyes held his in a look of surprised disbelief. '*You* are?'

'Yes, Talbotson was my mother's name before she married my father and became a Lovell, and Talbotson International is her inheritance to me. I have a few cousins who own bits of it, but it's my company over all. I just haven't changed the name, that's all.'

Regarding him helplessly, Leisal said, 'You are the most amazing man I've ever met, James.'

He laughed softly. 'Anyway, I'd been trying to think of a way to get back to you—your letters weren't very encouraging!'

'Neither were yours.'

'I wanted you to have some time; I didn't want to push you into anything you weren't ready for!'

'What has all this to do with Talbotson International, or Mr Talbotson, and your being here in Avignon?'

'I'm coming to that. When I heard about your money problems—and looking for some way to hold on to you—well, to put it bluntly, I've bought the company. In other words, Leisal Pavlova Leontina Adrianovitch—I'm your new boss!'

Acutely uncomfortable, Leisal could neither speak nor move. She looked into James's smiling eyes for several long moments, then she got up and slowly made her way across the room to pick up her bag from the table. She stood thoughtfully still with her back to him and James watched her with eyes filled with pleasure and torment, waiting for her reaction. When he could see the reaction he wanted wasn't forthcoming, he got up and moved towards her, coming up softly behind her and putting his arms around her waist.

'Is it so terrible?' he asked gently, his mouth against her ear.

She spun to face him, causing him to take a step back, the light from her expressive eyes glittering with anger. 'And am I part of the package deal?'

His eyes narrowed when he read her expression: this wasn't the reaction he'd planned at all. 'What the hell's that supposed to mean?'

Leisal made a circular movement with her arm, indicating the table for two, the soft lights, and now, through a half-open door, she could see the huge double-bed. 'Do you think

I'm a fool, James?' Her anger was blazing from her eyes. 'Am I part of the negotiations? Do I come with the company like a—like a filing cabinet?'

He looked at her in pure astonishment, shocked by the bitterness in her voice. 'You don't understand.'

'No,' Leisal said more quietly now, 'I don't. But I want you to know this, James, I don't come as part of any deal, and I'm not going to let you hurt me this way.'

She pulled away and walked to the door, closing her hand over the handle, but James moved with her and covered her hand with his, saying quietly, 'Leisal, please listen, it's not what you're thinking.'

She smiled sadly, looking up into his face. 'Isn't it, James? Then, for God's sake tell me what it is.'

There was a long silence, and his voice raw, he said, 'I love you, Leisal . . . I love you and I want you. I want to marry you. All I ever want is your happiness, and if it means buying your bloody TV company to ensure all that, then so be it.' Leisal felt his arms fold around her and she leaned against him, letting his love flow over her and soothe away all the anger and hurt pride that had filled her heart. She felt his mouth kiss her hair and his voice was muffled when he spoke again. 'Do you believe me, Leisal? Do you trust me?'

She lifted her face to his. 'It's against my

better judgement, but, yes, I think I do,' she replied softly, smiling at last. 'I really do.'

'Then will you marry me?'

Leisal put her arms around his back, feeling the crevice of his spine through the thin cotton of his shirt, and moving her fingers over the taut muscles on the incline of his shoulders. She shivered as his arms encircled her, strong, hard as iron, yet tender as a feather-touch. She felt a shudder of passion rack his body as he burrowed his mouth into the sweet-scented skin of her throat, bringing a tide of response flooding through her.

Half-formed thoughts whirled in her brain, settling into a meaningless disorder of which she could make no sense. 'And your aunt? Does she know how you feel about me?'

He drew a deep, harsh breath as his eyes slid over her. 'Come back to Hanaheen with me and find out for yourself.'

She made a small, involuntary movement. She would be deluding herself if she believed Harriet Lovell would welcome her with open arms. She loved him. And she was tempted, but she shook her head. She was aware of a small voice of doubt still tugging at her heart. She needed more time. 'I—I—have to finish the film,' she faltered.

His voice changed, becoming distant with remembered thoughts. 'How much time do you need?'

'I'm—I'm not sure.'

'Then I'll tell you. Two weeks more is all the time it will take. After that, you must make up your mind what you want to do, Leisal. I'll never push you into anything. When you're ready, I'll be waiting.' He was holding himself on a tight rein and she knew it, but his suddenly narrowed stare held her comprehension as he finished. 'Let's have dinner now.'

CHAPTER EIGHT

In the main reception room of the Grand Hotel, Avignon, the party was in full swing and Leisal edged her way towards the open doorway in the hope of taking a breather. Leaning against a pillar, she gazed around at the assortment of distinguished guests invited tonight to celebrate the end of filming *Sister of Judaea*, and breathed a sigh that was a mixture of relief and apprehension.

Tomorrow she was to leave this familiar life she knew so well; a life that had been part of her since she'd first learned to memorize a few lines at her grandmother's knee. And the hours of anguish she had suffered to reach the biggest decision of her life would soon be over. A decision already made even before Boushka's letter arrived this morning.

She turned smilingly to the man who came

to stand beside her. She could read him like a book and Tony was almost punch-drunk from the indications that his series was already a sensational success.

'Well, we made it,' he murmured almost to himself. 'We've got another smash-hit on our hands, Leisal. You should be over the moon instead of skulking in a corner like this. What's the matter with you?'

'Nothing's the matter,' she replied quietly, her eyes momentarily revealing a guarded defensiveness.

'Then cheer up, we've got a breakfast meeting lined up first thing tomorrow. We have to discuss the next series. Now that we've got all the money we'll ever need from Talbotson, we can really fly. Johnnie Lewestein's come up with a story that'll shake the viewing public like they've never been shaken before. It's terrific, and I can just see you as the lawyer defending the—'

'Tony—' Leisal held up a restraining hand to the director in an effort to gain his attention, 'Tony, I have to tell you something.'

'Tell me what?'

'I won't be available for the next film, you'd better start looking for someone else.'

Tony almost choked on his drink, visibly taken aback by her words. 'Not available? What the hell are you saying, Leisal, the part's tailor-made for you.'

She turned to face him. Tony was not a

good loser but Leisal had known him long enough to know how to handle him. She smiled and leaned closer to him, raising her voice to make herself clear above the buzz of conversation, the music, the laughter, and the clinking glasses. 'I was talking to Johnnie this morning about it and we both agree, Melinda Layton would be better in the part. Her image is—well—more serious than mine. She'd make a far better legal type than I would. She'll be absolutely right.'

'That's absolute rubbish! Image has nothing to do with it. What are you talking about? It's your face that makes them switch their tellys on.'

'I have other plans.'

'You're crazy, Leisal: you can't have other plans.'

'But I have, and don't try to talk me out of them because it won't work. I've already made my decision.'

Tony glared, his eyes at once suspicious and owl-like, as if he'd suddenly remembered something. He lit a cigarette and then asked flatly, 'And this momentous decision you've made—I don't suppose it has anything to do with that guy in Ireland?'

Leisal looked away, only the fine line of her drawn eye-brows giving away a spark of anger. 'The decision is my own and, with respect, Tony, it's none of your damn business.'

'Of course it's my business!' he insisted.

'Look at the facts, Leisal. You're on top of the world! You can command any salary you want! Why throw it away on some guy you've only known a few months? And—', he hesitated, looking at her with a queer little twisted smile, 'what about me? We're a good team!' But something in Leisal's expression silenced him and he took a swig of his wine sullenly. He paused again, looking at her oddly, then he went on, 'You've made up your mind then?'

'Yes.'

'Is there nothing I can say—or do—to make you change it?'

'Nothing.'

Tony looked around the room—it was stifling in spite of the air conditioning—then he said in a tired voice, 'Well, that's that then. I suppose if it's OK for you, then it has to be OK for me.'

Leisal turned to him, her expressive eyes wide and full of affection for her unpredictable old friend and director. 'Of course it'll be OK for you, you'll survive—you always do.' She smiled, then added as a small reminder that he had a wife to think about as well: 'And now that Suzanne is coming home soon, you have a wonderful future in front of you.'

'Leisal.'

'I must go now, I have some packing to do. Make my excuses will you, Tony?'

He held her eyes for several moments as if willing her to change her mind, but as he read her expression he merely nodded resignedly and bent his head to kiss her hand. 'If you ever need your job back—if things don't work out—you have my number?'

Leisal leaned forward and kissed his cheek. 'Yes, I have your number,' she smiled and gave him a fond wink, adding softly, 'I have a plane to catch tomorrow so if you'll excuse me, I'll have an early night. Goodbye, Tony, and good luck.'

'And good luck to you, Leisal, I think you might need it.'

*   *   *

As the plane took off she remembered James's words to her that night in Avignon—*take me on trust, just as I am, without question,*—and Leisal reasoned that she was doing exactly that. She trusted him implicitly. She had chosen to spend the rest of her life with James and not Harriet Lovell.

She changed planes at Heathrow and boarded the plane for Ireland. Far below she could make out the shimmering glint of the sea as they drew nearer to Shannon, and she felt her heart begin to lift as every mile took her nearer to James. Nearer to the feel of his arms holding her again, loving her.

Soon Leisal could see below her the rugged, claw-like coastline beyond Hanaheen, and the intermittent white crests of the waves as they rolled into the channel, separating the mainland with Dancer's Island. Soon the familiar towering forms of the Dancers themselves blurred into view. She felt suddenly at home.

Coming out of the passport control, she could see the tall, unmistakable figure of James scanning the crowds, waiting for her, his arm shading his deeply dark eyes from the sun. Her entire future was wrapped up in this lone tall figure who'd been watching the sky, waiting for her.

'Leisal, over here!'

Suddenly she was in his arms. Smiling down into Leisal's eyes, James could hardly believe his luck that she was back with him again. He loved the fire he saw in their tawny depths, and held her as though he'd never let her move from his side again. As they stood together in their embrace, his dark handsome looks in startling contrast to her striking tawny beauty, the rest of the world was lost to sight, and his eyes, as they looked into hers, were brilliant with love.

'Your grandmother told me you were on your way,' he murmured. 'She told me to meet you here, but I wasn't sure whether you'd be here or not.'

Arm-in-arm they went out to the car. Once inside, James placed his hands on to her shoulders and looked into her face a long time before he spoke. 'I was scared stiff in case you wouldn't come.'

'It's seemed like ages, James, like a thousand years.'

He nodded, 'I couldn't see your face—I tried and tried but I couldn't see it. I even tried to paint your picture while I waited for you.'

She gave him a delighted little smile. 'Did you, James? May I see it?'

He shrugged and shook his head. 'I couldn't do it. I had to give it up.'

'Why?'

'Because I couldn't see your face. It was as though I was blind with love. I don't think I'll ever be able to paint again, I'm too incoherent, and too unseeing for anything except the real flesh and blood of my girl.'

She reached her hand to his face, her heart bursting with overwhelming love and joy. 'Perhaps, one day when I'm old and fat, you'll be able to paint me then.'

'Would you like me to?'

'Yes.'

They both laughed and held each other close, then James slipped the clutch and they set off for Hanaheen.

They were almost there when James murmured softly at last, pointing his finger towards the ocean, 'Look, Leisal.'

She turned her head to see that the sun had moved around Dancer's Island, and a blinding golden shaft of light shone down upon the two stone statues. From this angle they seemed fused together, held in the rays of the sun; the dancers at one end of the shaft of sunlight and Leisal and James at the other; uncannily, as though the ghosts of the young monk and his lady were living again through their love.

'They're giving us their blessing, James.'

'Yes, I think they are. But this time, for us, there'll be no jealous husband to blow my head off, thank God.'

She turned her face to his, her eyes suddenly dark with questioning. 'You're right, there'll be no jealous husband, but what about jealous aunts? Does she know I'm back?'

'Yes.'

'And Enid, does Enid know, too?'

'Yes.'

'And how has your aunt taken it?'

James turned his head briefly. 'Are you afraid?'

'A little.'

He smiled, squeezing her hand reassuringly. 'There's no need to be.'

Leisal wished with all her heart she could share his confidence as the last few miles sped by. Never in all her days would she forget the exultant look in Harriet Lovell's face on the morning she left Hanaheen for France.

She wound down the window a little and took a long breath of sea air, asking softly, 'Did you ever wonder, James, why I cut my holiday short in that way?'

James didn't answer right away. Instead he

133

drew up against the side of the road, pulled on the hand-brake and regarded her sombrely. 'Yes, I wondered about it a lot. I thought for a while that you'd had enough of Hanaheen—and me—and I thought you wanted to get back to acting again. Was I mistaken?'

Leisal nodded. 'Yes. It was something else, something your aunt said to me. She—I know she wanted you to marry Enid and not someone like me.'

He turned his head sharply. 'What did she say that made you believe that?'

She told him of the day she'd been summoned to the old lady's room, and of the angry conversation that had passed between them.

When she had finished, James gave a hard little laugh. 'Why on earth didn't you say something? Why didn't you tell me she'd been giving you a rough ride?'

She shrugged vaguely. 'I didn't think it was any of my business at the time.'

He pulled his arm tighter around her shoulder. 'I can explain all that, come on, let's take a walk.'

James helped her climb out of the car. His hand slipped from her shoulder and grasped her hand as together they strolled along the edge of the cliff. Neither spoke, and when Leisal looked up into his face, turned upwards now, with his eyes screwed against the sun as he watched a white gull wheel in the air above them, he reminded her of a dark primitive god.

After a while Leisal asked, 'Is your aunt waiting for us at Hanaheen?'

'Yes.' He gave her a sideways look, a small smile playing around his mouth. 'Are you ready? It's time I introduced her to her future niece-in-law.'

Leisal looked out over the sea. She could well imagine the old lady's reaction to that nugget of information! But, Leisal gave a mental shrug, she'd made her decision to give up her career to marry James Lovell and she wasn't about to back away from it now—whatever consequences came of it. And there was just one more obstacle to overcome. Looking back at him she murmured lamely, 'I'm ready, James.'

As they walked together to the car she felt the strength of James filling her soul. Marriage to him would be wonderful and, in spite of what was to come, she knew she'd made the right decision. Only one question marred her contentment. It burned in her brain like a forest fire and she had a sudden sharp memory of Harriet Lovell's face wearing that triumphant look and that thin cold voice saying again: *You're not wanted here!*

Well, she *was* here whether the old lady liked it or not! And, what's more, she intended to stay!

She looked up at James and saw the corner of his mouth lifted into a smile. 'Don't worry,

Leisal. Everything will be all right.'

She smiled back wryly. Would it? How could he be so sure? The next couple of hours should be very interesting anyway, she thought grimly, climbing back into the car. Only one question was in her mind now. How would Harriet Lovell take the news?

CHAPTER NINE

As they reached Hanaheen and drove up the long gravel drive, Leisal could see a stable-boy exercizing one of the horses in the fields beside the wide expanses of emerald-green lawns. Everywhere was in full summer bloom. The distant blur of the Caha mountains was a sleepy haze of purple and grey, and even the trees seemed to be lifting their heavy branches in welcome. Hanaheen was so beautiful, and it was wonderful to be back; but in spite of all its beauty and the intense joy of being with James, Leisal wasn't looking forward to the next couple of hours at all.

The memory of the exultant look on Harriet Lovell's old face, when Leisal had made her departure for France almost three months ago, would burn forever in her memory, and try as she may to blot it out, it wouldn't leave her.

On the journey from the airport, Leisal had tried to find out from James exactly what had passed between him and the old lady, but in spite of her anxiety, James seemed reluctant to tell her anything of his aunt's reaction to the news that he intended to marry Leisal Adrian after all. And Leisal could only guess what that reaction had been.

There had been something odd in James's manner since they left the airport, and there was something very odd in his manner now. She had a vague feeling he was keeping something from her, but try as she might she couldn't imagine what it could be. His manner had been teasing, playful, and then tender and loving, and the last few hours had been the happiest of Leisal's life, and while they had been together not even the prospect of facing Harriet Lovell again had inhibited the joy she shared with James.

The late summer dusk was falling now and the sky was becoming streaked with orange and gold as the sun's reluctant departure below the horizon set its seal on a memorable day.

His grin as they stepped out of the car caught her attention again and she asked, 'What's the matter, James? What's so funny?'

He inclined his head to a black, old-fashioned car parked outside the main entrance to the house. 'Looks like we've got company.'

Leisal's gaze followed his and a small frown puckered her face. 'James, that car—I'm sure I recognize it—! Her heart sank like a stone. It was bad enough facing the old lady without this added complication. And today of all days. 'Perhaps it would be better if we came back later . . .'

James grinned even wider as he caught the look on her face, and he shrugged, catching her hand in his. 'Come on, let's get it over with. The car's a new one on me, let's see who it belongs to.'

'Do we have to, just now?'

'Yes, come on.'

They went inside the house. Bridget was arranging some flowers in a vase on a table by the staircase and looked up as they went in.

'Well, the saints be praised. I'm glad you've brought her back to Hanaheen, Mr James.'

'I told you I would, Bridget.' James squeezed Leisal's hand then asked the housekeeper, 'Is my aunt anywhere around?'

'Aye, that she is. She's in there.' Bridget nodded her head towards the conservatory door. 'There's someone with her—a lady—and a strange one at that. They've been in there these last two hours, and they seem to have a lot to say—talk, talk, talk. I took some tea in but I thought Miss Harriet would burst a blood-vessel, her face was as red as old Millory's shirt, and I could tell they were having one divil of a row.'

James looked at Leisal. 'Then I think perhaps we'd better go in and see what's going on.'

'If you think we must,' murmured Leisal quietly.

He opened the door of the conservatory and, taking her hand, he led her through. Harriet Lovell was standing by the half-open door that led into the garden, and the old lady turned her head as they entered, holding them in a quiet gaze.

It was a different kind of look in the china-blue eyes. One that Leisal hadn't seen before and it surprised her: it was a calm look, not defeated, but calm and resigned. James's arm stole softly around her shoulders, leading her further into the room, but she stopped suddenly as her eyes moved to Harriet's companion, and she recognized the tall figure standing by the table.

'*Boushka!*'

She moved forward quickly and instinctively towards her grandmother. The old lady gave a cry of joy and reached out her broad arms, hugging Leisal to her ample bosom. 'Dear Leisal,' the old lady murmured, tears glinting in her painted old eyes.

James watched as Leisal embraced her grandmother. He had never seen Pavla Adrian before and now stood fascinated as the unbelievably fantastic figure hugged Leisal.

The woman's presence was formidable. She was tall, stately, and her broad-hipped figure was clad in a flowing satin kaftan which rustled as she moved. Her grey hair was elegantly waved and coiled on top of her head. The piercing blue eyes, under their heavy make-up, swept Leisal up and down fondly and then they swung to James, staying on his face until Leisal at last broke free from her embrace and stood back emotionally.

'Boushka, remember I wrote and told you? This is James . . . James Lovell.'

The old actress scrutinized James for a long time; so long that James began to feel a little uncomfortable under the penetrating gaze. He knew she was sizing him up and would miss nothing about him. She gave a condescending nod of her coiffured head. 'Yes, I rather gathered it was.' She held out an elegant hand for him to kiss.

When the welcome had subsided, Leisal looked first at her grandmother and then at James's aunt. The two old ladies stood before them; one, tall and stately, and the other, tiny and thin: both of them frozen in time, clearly from another age, another world that had long ago ceased to exist.

'What's happening? What are you doing here, Boushka?' Leisal asked at last, her expression bewildered, believing she was dreaming all of this, and her grandmother was not really there at all. 'How did you know I would be here today?'

Before Pavla Adrian could answer, Harriet Lovell smiled and stepped forward from the window, and although the old cheeks were pale, for the first time Leisal saw a glimmer of warmth in the eyes of James's aunt.

'It's a long story, and something my nephew knows more about than he's admitting to,' Aunt Harry said, turning to James with a glint in her eye.

Leisal spun to face him with interest and surprise. 'You knew all the time that my grandmother was here, didn't you, James?'

He smiled, and kissed her on the cheek. 'I'll own up to it.' Then he moved across to kiss his aunt, adding quietly, 'I won't lie to you, Leisal. I wrote to your grandmother and asked her to come to Hanaheen.'

Harriet moved across the room. 'I think before I tell you what this extraordinary creature is doing here, we should all have some tea.'

'I think I could do with something a bit stronger than tea,' commented James drily.

In the drawing room, when tea had been cleared away, and the four of them were seated together, Aunt Harry began her explanation.

'It's difficult to know where to begin,' she said.

'It was always difficult, Harriet, from the moment we met. Best to start right at the beginning,' suggested Leisal's grandmother.

Harriet Lovell gave a small nod of her head, 'Yes, you're right, as always, Pavla.' She stared

141

blankly at the wall for a moment, as though seeing it all again in the blank space. 'Berlin . . .', she murmured, softly, 'Berlin was where it all started.'

The tale unfolded, and as it did, Leisal became engrossed as she listened to the two old ladies reliving their memories as they moved in and out of the past, recollecting incidents and long-faded memories, first one, and then the other.

Leisal's grandmother had been a young actress at the end of the war, and she had been sent to Berlin to entertain the Allied Armies after the city had been taken. At the same time, James's aunt, Harriet Lovell, was attached to the British Army as a driver for one of the generals, and it was there, in the beleaguered bombed-out ruins of Berlin that the two women had met. Two young, beautiful girls, each one so different in background and temperament to the other.

Harriet had met the young Russian officer first. He was different from the other soldiers—the son of a count, and his name was Nikki. He was young, charming, aristocratic and very handsome in his long-coated grey uniform and knee-high leather boots. His shoulders were broad and his eyes were as blue as a clear summer day. Nikki took her out every chance he could, and it wasn't long before Harriet realized she was hopelessly, crazily, in love with him.

One evening he came to pick Harriet up as usual, but this time he was very excited by the fact that he'd managed to get two tickets for a play that was on that night in the American zone. He desperately wanted to see the beautiful actress whose family had fled Russia many years before, and about whom he'd heard his family rave.

Harriet recalled how Nikki was bewitched by Pavla Adrian, and afterwards, in the little bar where Nikki and Harriet went for supper, to everyone's astonishment Pavla came in with a group of actors and American officers. Nikki was overwhelmed and insisted on an introduction, so, as Harriet knew most of the officers, and was anxious to please her handsome young officer, she was able to manoeuvre an invitation to Pavla's table.

It had been a momentous evening. They got along famously, the three of them, and during the next few weeks they saw a great deal of each other. Harriet and Pavla soon formed a close friendship and became so intimate that they were almost like sisters.

'Of course, the inevitable happened,' said Harriet, glancing at Pavla quickly. 'It was an impossible situation. I think Nikki loved us both. He was seeing me one night, assuring me of his undying devotion, and assuring Pavla of the same thing on the next.'

'I loved him so much,' murmured Pavla, 'I could have forgiven him anything.'

'Not quite anything,' said Harriet Lovell quietly. 'You see, neither of us realized that he was in love with the other. These things happen in wartime, everything is so transient, so ephemeral, one could love someone enough for a lifetime in a few short hours. Then people were moved on, sometimes at a moment's notice, and most romances fizzled out one way or another.' She smiled a little ruefully. 'But, unfortunately, in our ménage à trois, it became more complicated, more intense.'

'Indeed it did.' Leisal's grandmother shook her waved head somberly. 'And very tragic in the circumstances.'

Leisal felt James's arm slip across her shoulders and she lay back against him, loving the comfort of his arms, and waiting eagerly for the two old ladies to continue their story.

It was Pavla's voice that took up the threads. 'I remember finishing my performance one afternoon: I was in my dressing-room waiting for Nikki to call for me. I remember my door was open and, from the passage outside, I overheard one of the chorus girls talking of a wedding that was causing some excitement. Weddings always caused excitement in those days. Not many people took the chance, and there was always some difficulty with permission, and forms, and red-tape to get through. The authorities discouraged anyone from marrying in the forces, especially if the couple came from different countries—American, French, British, but particularly Russian—so when I heard Harriet's name mentioned, and then Nikki's, I couldn't believe—*wouldn't believe*—that it was true. How could he be marrying Harriet when he was in love with me?' She sighed deeply, remembering the painful moment. 'But it *was* true! And when I realized that, I was devastated—and angry.' Pavla Adrian went on softly. 'I thought there must be some mistake.' Her voice was so quiet now that it was almost inaudible and Leisal held her breath, waiting for her grandmother to continue. 'You see, Nikki had already promised to marry me . . . we'd even talked about the date.'

Harriet Lovell stared a long time at Pavla, her eyes clouded in memory. 'I remember that day well, Pavla. I remember you coming to my flat in the Heinestrasse, and asking me if it was true. I remember your face . . .'

'And were you going to marry him, Harry?' It was James who asked the question.

Harriet took a long, deep sigh, her old head shaking with the memory of that afternoon so long ago. 'Yes. We were . . .' She glanced again at Pavla. 'Oh, yes, I was going to marry him, I loved him very much.'

Leisal saw that her right hand was gripping and twisting the sapphire ring savagely as the old lady's tension grew.

'But you didn't,' James said softly.

145

'No, I didn't. You see', her voice faltered, 'I didn't know that Pavla was as much in love with him as I was. Close as we were we never talked of him in any way except as friends. I only found out her feelings for him when she asked me if our engagement was true, and I couldn't understand why she was so upset—I thought she would have been pleased for me . . .' The thin voice trailed off.

Pavla broke in quietly. 'I couldn't tell her why I was so upset—not then. Not when I saw how much she loved him. In fact, I couldn't tell her at all, so I just went away. In the end Nikki told her.' She turned away and went to stand by the fireplace. She stood motionless, the light from the window blurring her expression, making it unreadable.

'Couldn't tell her . . . ?' Leisal went to her grandmother's side and laid her hand over the wrinkled old one. 'What couldn't you tell her, Boushka?'

The two old ladies glanced at each other. Then Pavla took Leisal's hand in hers, inhaling deeply and saying softly, 'I couldn't tell her I was pregnant. That I was having Nikki's child.'

The silence in the room was deafening, and after a moment Leisal closed her hand around her grandmother's. Pavla Adrian's eyes looked into Leisal's and her voice, when she spoke again, was full of tender emotion. 'I was having Nikki's baby, and when Harriet found out about it soon afterwards, she—she went away ... she got herself transferred somewhere—far away from me and from Nikki.

'I couldn't bear it,' whispered Harriet. 'I had to get away. As far away as I could.'

Harriet Lovell got up and stood silently looking into the empty fire grate. Leisal looked from one old lady to the other, her eyes filled with emotion, 'What happened to the baby, Boushka?' she asked. 'What happened to you and your Russian soldier?'

Her grandmother stared at the thin back of her old friend for many moments before she went on. 'Nikki and I got married secretly in a village outside Berlin. A German pastor married us, and for a little while we were very happy, but, when Nikki's commanders heard of it they transferred him back to Russia ...' Pavla's eyes were bleak. 'We never saw each other again, although we both tried hard over the years.'

She closed her eyes and became very still, her memory still seeing the handsome young face of the soldier of her youth. Then James asked gently, 'Is he still in Russia as far as you know?'

Pavla shook her head. 'He died twelve years ago. At least they were considerate enough to let me know that much. I received a letter— well, hardly a letter. More of an official document I suppose you'd call it. It came from the embassy to inform me of his death. I

147

remember the message very clearly, it's burned into my heart. *Count Nikolas Ashkyov died peacefully on 2 October and we extend our condolences.*'

'And the baby?' Leisal urged softly. 'What happened to the baby?'

'Ah, yes, the baby. The beautiful daughter I had was your mother, Leisal.'

Leisal felt all her breath leave her body. She supposed she should have realized the fact but, even so, she couldn't speak for many moments. What agonies her grandmother must have been through! She had been their mainstay, her mother's and hers, and Leisal sat, remembering the times when she was a child, and the presents that had arrived for her from her grandmother. Whenever she had been at her lowest ebb, after her mother died, her grandmother had always been there, supporting her, loving her. She knelt softly by her grandmother's side. 'Thank you, Boushka, for all you've done for me—it can't have been easy. Oh, Boushka, thank you, thank you for so much.'

'And it was because you knew of all this that you responded to my letter and came today?' asked James. 'You knew that Leisal was going to marry Harriet Lovell's nephew?'

Pavla nodded. 'Yes, I'd always kept in touch with Harriet, although the relationship was a bit one-sided to say the least!' She gave a deep sigh. 'It was my idea that Leisal came here in the first place. I thought the peace and quiet of Hanaheen would do her a world of good after all that dreadful nonsense that had been in the press. I certainly didn't foresee a handsome young man like you, James, waiting in the wings to steal my granddaughter's heart. The few letters I've received from your aunt over the years didn't tell me anything about you. Then when I got Leisal's letter, the one she sent me before she went to France, I could see that this young man meant more to her than she was admitting. I could see that she was upset by the fact that James's aunt seemed set on breaking them up: but Leisal couldn't see the reason why. I did, though,' she admitted grimly. 'I understood why Harriet was so dead set against my granddaughter, and I thought it was time to do something about it. Then your letter came, James, and I knew that you loved my Leisal as much as she loved you. It was time to clear the air.'

Harriet Lovell turned to face them. 'Almost like history repeating itself, eh, Pavla?' She paused, looking from one to the other, adding softly, 'I think perhaps it's my turn to say something now.'

She moved over and sat down again, looking at Pavla with a smile, and then her eyes met Leisal's. She began softly, 'When I realized that Nikki loved Pavla more than he loved me, I was angry and bitter. She was so beautiful and talented, in a way that I could never be, and when I knew she was expecting his child I couldn't bear it. I had to get out of Berlin as soon as I could. I'd loved Pavla like my sister. I'd trusted her. And I knew she didn't know the depth of my feelings for Nikki. How could she, when I would never admit it to anyone, not even myself? I became full of bitterness. I hated all men, and, especially, I hated all actresses. I've lived all these years with that hatred eating away inside me. When you came here, Leisal,' her voice softened as she looked into Leisal's face, 'I saw Nikki again in your face—you're very like him, you know. I truly believed that you would deceive James as I'd convinced myself your grandfather deceived me, and I was prepared to do anything to stop you marrying him.' She held out a thin, bony hand to Leisal. 'How cruel and spiteful I've been, both to you and James. Will you ever be able to forgive me?'

Leisal got up and went to kneel beside the withered, bitter old lady who had caused so much anger, and pain. She looked into Harriet Lovell's eyes, and for the first time she saw how sad she must have been all these years.

'Of course you're forgiven,' Leisal assured her softly. 'Somehow, and in a way I can't explain, I always felt I understood.'

Pavla Adrian got up and put out her arms to Harriet Lovell. 'It's all a long time ago, Harriet, it's high time we put it behind us and started living again.'

Harriet nodded, her arms reaching out and clasping Pavla's, smiling at the woman who stood before her. 'Yes, it is—high time. Now I believe we have a wedding to arrange for my nephew and your granddaughter.'

Leisal felt James's arm tighten on hers, then he took a small step forward and turned a blindingly radiant smile upon the two old ladies. 'Aunt Harry . . . Boushka . . . I love you both, and no one is more pleased than I that all the old skeletons have been laid to rest.' He turned back to Leisal, taking her hand in his and holding it flat between his own, saying quietly, 'But with the greatest of respect to you, our wedding is something Leisal and I want to arrange for ourselves.'

Aunt Harry took a small step towards them, a faint red tinge appearing on her neck. Old habits die hard, thought Leisal, and Boushka held a restraining arm on Harriet Lovell's, holding her back and saying approvingly, 'It's their time now, Harriet.'

Harriet looked at James and then at Pavla with sombre eyes and a flickering smile. 'You're right, Pavla, and I'm sorry, James . . .' Then she added softly, 'I'm so sorry.'

James's black eyes focused on his aunt with unnerving intensity. 'Didn't I tell you, aunt, how much Leisal means to me? And didn't I tell you that, no matter what, I would have her as my wife?' His aunt nodded slowly as he continued, 'And didn't I tell you that you need

151

never be sorry for anything?'

Harriet Lovell closed her eyes for a brief moment, and then she opened them with a smile. 'Bless you both.'

James led Leisal from the room, leaving the two old ladies to reminisce, and they walked together into the garden. They walked in silence, each trying to drag themselves out of the past, out of the time of long ago, and back into their own sweet world of today and of tomorrow.

Leisal could hear the soft whinnying of the horses from the stables, and James's arms closed around her as they stopped by the white-painted gates. He kissed her tenderly and held her to his chest.

'Did you mind, Leisal?'

She looked up into his face, but the soft evening light was concealing the darkness of his eyes and she couldn't see the expression in their depths. 'Mind what, James?'

'Mind my telling them that we'll make our own arrangements?'

She smiled and laid her head back against his chest. 'Of course I didn't mind.'

'About the wedding, Leisal . . .'

'Yes?'

'I've managed to get the licence—would ten o'clock in the morning be all right with you?'

Leisal caught her breath and looked up again into his face. '*Tomorrow?*'

'Do you mind?'

'It's rushing it a bit, isn't it?'

'I don't think so. Why wait any longer than we have to?'

Leisal laughed. 'Why not, indeed. I suppose the honeymoon's all arranged, too, isn't it?'

He pulled her closer. 'I thought we'd spend some time on the island.'

'Oh, yes . . . the island.'

His finger traced the outline of her cheek and Leisal felt the reassurance of his closeness, the warmth of his body as he stood pressed against her. 'Are you cold, love?'

Leisal's breath caught in her throat. 'No, I'm not cold, how could I be beside you?'

He laughed softly, covering her face with his kisses. 'Lean closer to me and I'll keep you warm.' Then he put his hand into his pocket and brought out a small box, handing it to her. 'Here, my love, take this gift from my heart.'

She opened the box to find an emerald ring, glittering now in the late afternoon sun, and she slipped it on. It was the most beautiful ring she had ever seen. 'James, how beautiful,' she murmured softly. 'I'll wear this ring to my dying day to show the world my love.' She kissed him again, then laughed softly, shaking her head, 'I swear I'll never sleep tonight.'

His lips were warm against her hair. 'Come closer, and I'll show you a most pleasurable way to sleep.'

CHAPTER TEN

Leisal opened her eyes and lay for a full two minutes, reluctant to move. In the four weeks of their marriage she had not yet grown accustomed to the joy she felt on waking to find James by her side.

She turned her head towards him now, leaning over and kissing his temple as he lay sleeping. The corner of his lip curved but he didn't open his eyes, seeming content to receive Leisal's soft caresses and feeling the gentle stroke of her hand on his hair. James smiled, saying nothing, the silence of their embrace said more than a million words could ever do. Then, caught up in the same mutual tide of love, they searched for each other's lips.

James lifted the sheet up around them, kissing her cheek as he did so. 'Happy, Leisal?' She felt his mouth against her face, and she felt the soft breath of his laughter as he asked softly, 'No regrets?'

'No regrets, James.' She laid her head back against his shoulder. 'I've never been so happy in my life, and, James, I've been thinking . . .'

'What about?'

'About Hanaheen.'

'Mm?' His fingers were twining through her hair and she turned her head to kiss his finger-tips.

'I was reading that book on breeding while you were out exercizing the new foal yesterday!'

He burst out laughing. 'Book on breeding? Why, love, do you think we'll need to read about it? Are we expecting to hear the sound of tiny feet so soon?'

'Not that kind of breeding.'

'What other kind is there?'

'James, be serious. I was thinking about us buying more horses and trying to breed for the hurdles—perhaps even the National one day.'

He pulled himself up onto his elbow, his dark eyes teasing at first and then becoming serious as he saw that she meant what she was saying. 'Would you like to do that?'

'Yes, very much.'

'OK, love, when we get back on to the planet Earth again, we'll see what needs to be done.'

'I know we can do it.'

'We can do anything as long as we're together, Leisal.'

She reached her hand up to his face and let her fingers trace the tiny scar above his lip, whispering softly, 'I know, James. There isn't anything we can't do.'

He looked down into her face, seeing her parted lips raised and waiting for his kiss. He lowered his mouth to hers and his mouth was warm, tasting sweetly of wine, and she inhaled deeply the scent of his skin against her body.

His kiss was gentle, holding more tenderness than passion, and when it was over they held each other as if afraid to break the wonder of the moment.

They lay together in a shaft of brilliant sunlight, and outside the window, Leisal could hear the waves as they rolled against the sand, and knew instinctively that their love was protected from the world by the rock statues of the dancing lovers of Dancer's Island. Lovers who had given James and Leisal their blessing when they'd first come to the island as husband and wife just a few short weeks ago.

After a time, she heard James say her name softly, and she parted her lips, inviting him to take her as he desired. It was an invitation he chose not to resist.

His eyes were dark, darker even than she could remember, and the love that shone from them as he looked into her face took her breath away. He traced her lips with his tongue, and she could feel her response mounting again to the touch of his hand on her thigh, and his voice when he spoke was filled with love.

'I promise you, Leisal Pavlova Leontina Adrianovitch Lovell, I promise that I shall never give you cause to regret one moment with me . . . never—for as long as I live.'